"I'm not in the mood," Pansy warned

Her back was pressed against the door, her arms crossed over her chest in a way that only served to accentuate full breasts. Everything about her—her high color, her sparkling green eyes—bespoke passion. "You look *very* much in the mood," Rex murmured in correction. His fingers touched her lips.

"I've got a headache," she assured him.

His eyes twinkled. "Ah. Good thing I'm here. I'm good with headaches."

"Good at causing them," she said breathlessly as his hand crept around the back of her neck and began kneading the skin.

They were amazing together. Driven by desire, Rex inched closer, and because he'd stiffened with arousal, the firm bulk curved against her mound. A soft panting moan filled his ears, and when he glanced down, he saw that her nipples were erect beneath her shirt.

"This—" Pansy's eyes darted around the room, as if searching for a word "—affair we're having..."

"Is wonderful," he finished, his voice hushed with need as he feathered kisses against her cheek. He felt her knees weaken.

"Crazy," she corrected, turning languid in his arms.

"No..." The words were out before he knew what he was saying. "I'm falling in love with you."

Dear Reader,

I'm so excited to bring you #883 *The Seducer*, the second book in my BIG APPLE BACHELORS miniseries!

The series, including #875 *The Hotshot* and the final book #891 *The Protector*, involves three sexy brothers who also happen to be New York City cops. When their mother wins the lottery, she strikes up a deal: if each brother marries within three months, she'll split the winnings among them. While each book stands alone, much-loved characters are revisited in each story, and you'll get to see their lives progressing.

This month, you'll meet Rex Steele, an undercover master of disguise who has more on his mind than sex with a beautiful woman—or does he? When his father disappears, Rex travels to an island to find him...and then finds himself seducing a local woman in the dunes!

I know how much I've loved writing these books, so I do hope you'll continue to enjoy the Steele brothers' sensual adventures!

Very best,

Jule McBride

Meet all of New York's finest
in the BIG APPLE BACHELORS miniseries!

Truman is *The Hotshot* in April 2002
Rex is *The Seducer* in June 2002
Sullivan is *The Protector* in August 2002

Jule McBride
The Seducer

HARLEQUIN®

TORONTO • NEW YORK • LONDON
AMSTERDAM • PARIS • SYDNEY • HAMBURG
STOCKHOLM • ATHENS • TOKYO • MILAN • MADRID
PRAGUE • WARSAW • BUDAPEST • AUCKLAND

ISBN 0-373-25983-2

THE SEDUCER

Copyright © 2002 by Julianne Moore.

This edition published by arrangement with Harlequin Books S.A.

® and TM are trademarks of the publisher. Trademarks indicated with
® are registered in the United States Patent and Trademark Office, the
Canadian Trade Marks Office and in other countries.

Visit us at www.eHarlequin.com

Printed in U.S.A.

_____Prologue_____

TURN BACK! Pansy Hanley's instincts silently commanded. "If you don't quit following him, he's going to turn around and catch you," she chastised in a whisper. "And then you're going to feel like an idiot." Nevertheless, her eyes remained riveted on the strong, broad back of the dark-haired, dark-eyed stranger she'd been tailing along deserted Sand Road. He was moving in the shadows, his rolling gait slow, easy and oddly compelling. Everyone else on Seduction Island was still at the town meeting, and the souvenir shops and T-shirt kiosks were closed, the windows dark, the silhouettes of clouds overhead dancing mysteriously across the sidewalks.

"The guy's just a tourist," Pansy assured herself, but even as she spoke the words, she felt sure—maybe even hoped—they were a lie. Something—maybe the romance of the dark velvet night or the magic of the moon and stars—was convincing her that this stranger was the man of her dreams. Quite literally, since he was the spitting image of a dashing, irresistible pirate ghost who'd been sketched years ago by Pansy's ancestor and who was said to haunt the nearby dunes.

Not that the man was really a ghost, of course. "The guy's probably looking for someplace open so he can buy shells," Pansy assured herself nervously, trying to ignore the night's sensual, romantic aura. Far off, waves crested. Breakers crashed onto the beach, and the sea breeze blew strands of honey hair across her cheeks, bringing the taste of salt to her lips...a taste that could have been the stranger's bare skin. Just as she sighed, sinking against the sun-warmed, concrete side of a building, she realized the stranger was starting to head toward the dunes.

Lit by the yellow glow of a three-quarter moon, the majestic sand of the drifts swept upward, casting long dark shadows. As the gorgeous man walked into them, his body seemingly dematerializing and fading into darkness, he appeared oblivious of the peaking bluffs just above his head. Pansy's heart skipped a beat. Not so much because he was so tall, or so strong, with lanky, sinewy limbs and well-defined muscles, but because, with his flowing black hair and devastating eyes that had captured hers a few minutes before in the town meeting, he really was a dead ringer for Jacques O'Lannaise, the pirate who'd haunted Pansy's dreams and inspired her fantasies for years, ever since she'd first heard his name. Jacques had been the lover of Pansy's ancestor, Iris, and after Iris was tragically lost at sea, Jacques was said to have begun walking the dunes at night, searching for Iris as if he was hoping to find her and make wild love to her in the sand.

Pansy tried to chuckle, but the effort only produced a shiver of excitement and a soft, strangled hitch of breath. "At least Vi and Lily don't know I'm out here, following a tourist," she muttered, hoping the mention of her sisters might lend some reality to the situation. After all, her sisters would never let her live this down. Pansy was usually the most commonsensical

Hanley sister, but when it came to Jacques O'Lannaise...

"It can't be him," she whispered insistently. She was being ridiculous! Pirate ghosts didn't exist! Her breath quickened with anticipation anyway. If she didn't get a move on, she'd lose this guy! Pulled as if by the tides, she speeded her steps, unable to shake the uncanny sense that meeting him face-to-face was...well, somehow necessary. Destiny, she thought.

"You're really going crazy," she whispered. She was out here on a dark night following a stranger. She just hoped he didn't turn around. Of course, if he did, she could go home, climb into a hot sudsy tub and relax with a good book because he'd turn out to be your average vacationing tourist. Probably married and cruising Sand Road to buy T-shirts for his kids. Yes, once he turned around, Pansy would get a better look at him, and he'd no longer bear a resemblance to Iris's sketches of Jacques O'Lannaise.

But what was Pansy supposed to do if she caught up to him? She swallowed hard. She knew what she wanted to do.

Live her fantasies. She imagined strands of his hair brushing her cheeks as his lips lowered for a kiss, how hot his gaze would feel on her bare skin as they laid in the sand and removed their clothes. She pushed aside the thoughts, then gasped. He was stopping! Slowly, he turned, and as he did, his hair rippled. It was gorgeous, like dark waters into which someone had dropped a pebble. Awareness flooded her. "No," Pansy protested when he didn't turn enough to make his face visible in the darkness. For a second, she could swear he crooked a finger in her direction, but of course, he hadn't. "Turn all the way around," she urged, even more determined to catch him. The man really was the spitting image of the pirate who'd long been a part of the Hanley family legacy. Pansy couldn't let him get away. He headed into the strange, surreal, craterlike dunes, as if he knew she would follow him, as if he wanted to make love....

And then the man seemed to vanish.

1

One week ago...

AS SHE SWUNG OPEN the carved oak door to the New York brownstone she shared with her husband and where she still tidied her three sons' rooms daily even though they'd long ago left home, Sheila Steele felt the sticky summer heat gust inside, dislodging loose gray strands from her pinned-up hair. Anxiously smoothing them, in case this was another officer asking her to come to police headquarters to talk about her husband, Augustus's, disappearance, she peered out, heart clutching.

When she saw the man on the stoop, her heart sank. A lost tourist, she decided, taking in the khaki shorts, Hawaiian print shirt and shaggy blond hair. Dark blue eyes surveyed her from behind black-framed glasses, and a camera was slung around his neck. As a female New Yorker related to four cops, Sheila was safety conscious to a fault, and so, despite her husband's disappearance, which was consuming her with worry, she was also regretting that she'd be unable to let this poor stranger inside to use the phone, if that's what he wanted. He looked honest, like the kind of young man who'd get robbed on city streets if he wasn't careful. "Can I help you?"

He squinted. "Ma? It's me, Rex."

Her lips parted in frank astonishment. "I didn't even recognize my own son!" Underneath the disarming attire, her son Rex was as dark and swarthy as a pirate.

"I came as soon as Sully called with the news about Pop."

Sheila pressed a hand to her heart as her middle child stepped into the foyer, giving her a hug and kissing her cheek. "Don't feel bad about not recognizing me," added Rex, who'd worked undercover for years. "Nobody does, you know. That's the point."

Despite the circumstances of the meeting, Sheila leaned back to study the son who most shared her passions and temperament. "Hard to believe the tall, dark, handsome man I gave birth to is really under that costume somewhere."

"He is," Rex assured. Without the wig, contact lenses and cheek pads, he had dark unruly hair and hazel eyes that shifted between shadowy, moody colors—gray, blue and green. His cheeks were shallow, his lips full, his body sculpted from the hours he spent in the precinct gym. "My big case broke yesterday," he explained, "so I spent this morning riding the F train." The Mr. Nice Guy outfit was designed to make him an appealing target for pickpockets who rode the subway, hoping to fleece tourists.

Sheila managed a watery smile. Under other circumstances, she would have laughed. "My son," she murmured. "The professional victim. How many times have you been robbed this morning, sweetie?"

"Three," Rex admitted. "But I arrested them all, Ma."

"Good for you." She took a deep breath. "Well, c'mon inside. Everybody else is in the courtyard."

He followed her down a long hallway. "Everybody?"

"Both your brothers. Sullivan got here first. And Truman brought the woman he's been dating, Trudy Busey."

"The one I met the other day at lunch? From the *New York News?*"

Sheila nodded. "Truman was with her at the newspaper when I called him." Sheila grasped Rex's hand for support. "I'm so glad you're here."

"Pop's gonna be fine," he said, his voice reassuringly soft and yet grimly masculine, his eyes focused on the summery light at the end of the hallway. Through a screen door, riotous leaves sprawled in a courtyard garden that was one of Sheila's passions.

"I can't imagine what's happened to your father." She sighed. "You were supposed to go on vacation tomorrow, right?"

"To Seduction Island. Just off Long Island."

"That's where the boat was anchored before it..."

Exploded. Rex didn't blame her for not wanting to voice the word. "Pop knew I was going there as soon as my case broke."

"Maybe he wanted to meet you there," she probed, her voice catching. "Are you sure he didn't tell you why he was going there? Or who he was going with? Did he say anything about what he's involved in?"

"Nothing." Augustus Steele had begun his career as a beat cop in Hell's Kitchen, graduated to arresting gangs in Chinatown, then landed a job in administration at Police Plaza. Since he no longer worked cases, no one knew how he could have wound up aboard a boat that exploded near Seduction Island, New York. Or where he'd gone afterward. If he lived. Rex pushed aside the thought.

"If he needed help," Rex murmured, trying to ignore how much it hurt to admit it, "Pop would have gone to Truman or Sully. You know that, Ma." In the deepening warmth of her gaze, Rex felt her quiet understanding. He and his father had never really bonded. "I'll do whatever I can," he continued. "This is Pop we're talking about. Starting tomorrow, I've got a month off."

Dismay was in her voice. "But your vacation..." She knew Rex lived for the times when he fled to unknown beaches, often registering in hotels under assumed names so no one but her could find him. For one month a year, he pursued interests unlike those of his father, brothers and many Manhattan law enforcement officers—reading, writing, painting and cooking. Hobbies he loved, but that, in the Steele household, had often gotten him pegged as a sissy by his father. Not that his dad didn't love him, but Augustus had strict ideas about what constituted manhood, none of which involved interests in the arts.

"My vacation doesn't matter," Rex replied, wishing he could take the uncertainty from his mother's eyes. "Family first," he assured. "C'mon. Let's see what Sully's found out."

It wasn't good, Rex realized, after seating his mother and himself at a round table shaded by a leafy oak. He glanced at Truman, who'd come in his uniform, then at their oldest, suit-clad brother, Sullivan, who was captain of the precinct nearest the house.

Both brothers, with their light brown hair and whiskey eyes, were the spitting image of Augustus. Rex looked like Sheila. Her hair had been as dark as his before it turned gray.

"My boss Dimi's refusing to run the article I've been writing about your family and the NYPD," Trudy was saying, her blue eyes snapping with indignation, her straw-blond hair blowing across her cheeks with the breeze. "It was supposed to be in tomorrow's *News,* but Dimi won't publish anything until he's sure Mr. Steele's done nothing wrong." She groaned in frustration. "I can't believe this! Now, more than ever, your names should be in the paper! We need to figure out what's happened!"

Rex squinted at his brother's girlfriend, who was a reporter. Along with the news about Augustus, Rex had been apprised that Trudy and Truman had just cracked what the tabloids had dubbed the Glass Slipper Case. Judging from the light in Trudy's eyes when she glanced at Truman, she'd fallen for him while they were working together. Despite the circumstances, Rex felt a rush of happiness for his baby brother. "What was the article about?"

"For the past two weeks, Trudy's been on a ride along in the patrol car with me," Truman explained, rising from her side. He started pacing, the hands on his hips slipping down to a billy club and holstered gun. "That's how we wound up solving the Glass Slipper Case. Anyway, the article was supposed to be good PR for the city. You know, a day in the life of a cop. It was going to press tonight."

"I remember you mentioning it," said Rex.

"I was at my desk writing it," Trudy added, "as

well as the Glass Slipper story, when Sheila called."
Pausing, her eyes darted to Sheila's. "I'm sorry I was
so angry when I came over earlier today."

Rex was less concerned with what had transpired
between the women than with collecting facts pertain-
ing to his father's disappearance. "You say they're
pulling the story?"

Truman nodded, stepping behind Trudy, placing
his hands on her shoulders and massaging them. "The
rumor's that Pop's on the take."

"Ridiculous!" Sheila exclaimed. "Earlier, when
Trudy came over, I'd just gotten a call from Police
Plaza. They didn't even do me the courtesy of coming
by the house to tell me he disappeared! And he's been
on the force thirty-three years! He's never taken a
dime, except from his paycheck, but they made me go
all the way downtown to tell me he's...he's..."

Rex's fingers closed over hers. "It's okay, Ma."

Looking unconvinced, Sully thrust both hands deep
into his trouser pockets and relaxed against an oak
tree. Red painted lines on the bark marked their
heights as kids, but Sully, now thirty-six, towered
over the marks. "That internal affairs woman who's
been on my back is heading up the investigation."

Rex cursed under his breath. "Judith Hunt?"

"Yeah," returned Sully. "According to her, the
money in the city's Citizen's Contribution fund is
missing. She took a crew to Seduction Island to dive
for whatever's left of the boat."

"The Citizen's Contribution fund was set up so that
private citizens could make personal donations to the
police without any question of impropriety," said
Trudy.

"Do they really think your father could steal public money?" whispered Sheila. "After all his years of loyalty and service?"

Sully sighed, his eyes lighting briefly on his brothers. "I hate to have to say this, but they've got Pop withdrawing money at the bank. On videotape."

Sheila was dumbfounded. "Your father withdrew money?"

Sully paused, then said, "In light of some of the tragedies we've had in Manhattan, the account's bigger than ever. It was...seven million."

Sheila was reeling. "Dollars? Of public money? And a bank let him take it? There's got to be a mistake! He'd never..."

"He wire transferred the money from Citicorp," countered Sully, "then picked it up elsewhere in two suitcases. He works with the accounts, so he knew the numbers."

Sheila stared. "He took the money in suitcases? That's impossible. Your father could never do such a thing. He's an officer. He knows how that would look."

"The videotape's incriminating," agreed Sully.

Stricken, Sheila whispered, "What if he's dead?"

"C'mon now," chided Rex gently. "Pop's too tough to die."

"You've got a point there, Rex," agreed Truman.

"We'll figure this whole thing out," Sully assured.

"I just don't get it," interjected Trudy, lifting her hands to twine them with Truman's. "He's an administrator at Police Plaza. He doesn't even work on cases. The only logical explanation is that he stumbled onto something."

Rex raised an eyebrow. "Such as?"

Trudy shrugged. "Who knows?"

Rex rifled a hand through the blond wig he wore, wishing it didn't itch in the summer heat. "Even if Pop discovered someone mishandling funds—say, from the Citizen's Action account—taking the money himself is a strange way of fixing the problem. He had to know he'd be seen on tape. Maybe he posed intentionally," Rex mused. "Why wasn't the money invested, anyway? Isn't that the responsibility of the Dispersion Committee?"

Sullivan shrugged. "All good questions, Rex. But the fact is, we haven't got any real clues as to what's happened. Not yet. All anybody knows for certain is that the boat, named the *Destiny*, docked at the Manhattan Yacht Club and Pop was on deck when it left the slip."

Rex visualized the mile-long sidewalk fronting Battery Park, overlooking the Hudson River and the Statue of Liberty. "On Wall Street?" he murmured, imagining his father exiting Police Plaza, then walking along Centre Avenue. To get to the yacht club, he'd have passed City Hall, the Brooklyn Bridge and the Stock Exchange. "That's a pricey place to dock. Donald Trump and Henry Kravis keep boats there. Who owned it?"

"Registered under a false name," supplied Sullivan. "I'm still looking."

Rex shook his head. "We need to find that out."

"And if your father's still alive," added Sheila shakily.

"No bodies have been recovered," Rex reminded. When everyone fell silent, Rex cast brooding eyes into the garden, long enough that his gaze unfocused, making the world appear to be a blur of color. Situated on Bank Street in the West Village, the Steeles' home had been handed down through Sheila's family, and from the front, despite cheerful green shutters, the stone edifice was gloomy. The courtyard opened onto another world, however. Hidden from the city streets, the garden exploded with the flowers Sheila tended whenever she had spare time left after community work.

Silently, Rex cursed his father. Why didn't he bother to notice how often his wife's face was drawn with worry? She'd strived so hard to make their lives wonderful. And now this. Staring into the courtyard where they had played as kids, Rex could hear his father saying, "We've got to toughen you up, Rex. When you join the force, we don't want them thinking you're a pansy, do we?"

Nope. Which is why Rex had turned out as tough as shoe leather. He had a scar from a knife fight on the Lower East Side. A black belt in karate. Promotions for daring feats of courage. Commendations. He could outshoot any officer in Manhattan. But deep down, he was a lover, not a fighter. It was he, not his brothers, who remembered his mother's worry when Augustus didn't make it home from stakeouts. And the excruciating times—sometimes minutes, sometimes hours—between hearing a cop was killed in the line of duty, then being told the victim wasn't Augustus. No doubt, things were as Trudy said. Augustus had discovered wrongdoing, then set out in high macho style to catch the perpetrator himself.

Now Rex would have to find him. *A far cry from the*

last time Ma called us here, Rex thought ruefully. Only a few weeks ago, she'd received one of the biggest lottery wins in New York City history, and driven by a good heart and desperate desire to see her sons happily married, she'd made an unthinkable deal. If Sullivan, Rex and Truman kept silent about the money and married within three months, she'd divide fifteen million dollars between them. Otherwise, she'd give the money to a wildlife research station on the Galapagos Islands.

She'd looked so beautiful that day, too, with humorous lights dancing in her eyes. Unlike the stiff gray suit she'd chosen for today's trip to Police Plaza, she'd been wearing a vest embedded with tiny mirrors and a brightly patterned skirt, dressed for her volunteer work with CLASP, an organization for the homeless.

Rex could still hear what Truman had to say once the men were alone. "Fifteen million! That's five million each."

Sully had shaken his head. "If Ma hadn't shown us the letter from the lottery board, I wouldn't have believed something like this could happen."

Rex had chuckled. "Don't be so suspicious, Sully. This is Ma we're talking about. Not a criminal."

"Beg to differ," Truman had countered. "Didn't Ma say she expects us to find wives? And if we don't, she's going to give all that money away to a foundation that saves sea turtles?"

"They also save marine iguanas," Rex had reminded.

"And don't forget flightless cormorants," Sully had said.

"Oh, right," Truman had whispered. "Flightless cormorants."

At that, the brothers had stared at each other in shock and, a moment later, they were hooting—clapping each other's backs and wiping tears of merriment from their eyes.

But Rex had meant what he'd said. As far as he was concerned, the Galapagos Islands could have the money. Like his brothers, he'd been weaned on stories of the mysterious volcanic islands just off the coast of Ecuador. Close to a mainland rich with a history of Inca warriors, Amazon explorers and Spanish conquistadors, nature had been left to thrive on the islands, becoming home to wildlife that existed nowhere else on earth. Rex had spent more than one summer vacation lounging on the rocky beaches, sketching the animals.

"We can't find soul mates in three months," he'd argued that day, intrigued by their mother's inventive way of encouraging them to find spouses.

"She said wives, not soul mates," Truman had argued.

But for Rex, they were the same. Besides, to him marriage was just a piece of paper. Maybe because he was a lawman, he wanted something that transcended legalities. He wanted mystery. Romance. Poetry. Soul-searing sex. A lover whose warm body would twine with his, melting his heart. Each year, on his annual sojourn, he imagined he might find that woman. He envisioned meeting her while wandering in the dunes near a deserted beach and making love to her in the hot sand while sea foam washed over their bare bodies.

Not that it mattered. Sure, he'd love to see his mother's face light up with the news that he'd found someone, but Augustus was missing, which meant Rex would be looking for him on Seduction Island—not love.

Rex said a silent goodbye to the month-long hiatus he got once a year. At least he'd already forwarded his mail to Casa Eldora, the two-bedroom cottage he'd rented on Seduction Island in the name Ned Nelson. According to the sexy-voiced Realtor whose laughter sounded like crystal bells and who had introduced herself as Pansy Hanley, the waterfront place was on stilts, its shingles weathered to silver. It was nestled where sand drifts gave way to otherworldly, deeply cratered dunes. Accessible by a private shell road, the house was off the main drag, Sand Road, but still in view of the ocean.

How many times had he spoken to Pansy? Rex couldn't recall. But they'd established an easy rapport. When they met, Rex had been planning to do what he always did on vacation—drop the mask. Lose the disguises. Trade in his sidearm for a fishing rod. He'd ask Pansy Hanley to Casa Eldora for dinner...maybe more. Now he squeezed his mother's hand. "If Pop's out there, I'll find him, Ma. Don't worry."

No doubt, he'd be busy on Seduction Island, just not seducing. So much for this year's hopes that Pansy Hanley might turn out to be a dream lover.

"PANSY? LILY? Are you home yet? We've got to talk!"

Long before she saw her youngest sister, Violet, Pansy Hanley registered her high-pitched voice and instinctively double-checked the jacket to the all-white suit she'd slung around the back of a kitchen chair to make sure it was safe from Vi. Vi, when excited, was the world's biggest klutz, and Pansy wanted to wear the jacket to meet her client, Ned Nelson. "I'm here," Pansy called toward the screen door, waiting for Vi to appear in the dunes. "Lily just got home, too—"

"I know it was my turn, so thanks for making lunch," said Lily, breezing into the kitchen and plopping down at the table. "I was running late."

As Pansy washed down a bite of her specialty—almond butter on homemade rye—she studied her sister's string bikini. "If you get bored on the beach, Lily," Pansy offered dryly, "you can always take off your bathing suit and play cat's cradle."

Lily chuckled. "Or hog-tie the nearest beachcomber, rub him down with Coppertone and force him to have sex with me."

Pansy tried to look scandalized. "Your mind's in the gutter, Lily."

Lily merely grinned. "Too bad every guy out there with a metal detector is pushing seventy and too old for us. What's Vi so upset about?"

"Who knows?" Pansy shrugged as Vi pushed through the screen door, lifting a shoulder bag stuffed with mail onto the kitchen table. "You're a mess," gasped Pansy, taking in Vi's mail carrier uniform—a striped shirt and gray shorts—splashed with syrupy pink liquid. Pansy's eyes dropped to the soda can in Vi's hand just as Vi crushed her stubby-nailed fingers around it.

"Don't tell me," quipped Pansy. "We're fresh out of boards you can crack with your head."

Ignoring the good-humored gibe, Vi set aside the

crushed can and lifted the remaining sandwich. Between healthy, gulping bites, she said, "Thanks for lunch. I've got to change uniforms, so I've only got a minute."

It was hard to say how the same gene pool turned out three such different females. All the Hanleys had light brown hair, just a shade down from honey blond, but Pansy's flowed in sumptuous layers past her shoulders. The curviest of the three, she liked wearing a trace of makeup and comfortable skirts, practical but feminine, nothing she'd have to iron. Today's white suit was an anomaly, chosen because the client she was to meet, Ned Nelson, had sparked her imagination during their phone conversations, though she wasn't quite sure why.

By contrast to Pansy, the middle sister, Lily, owner of Lily's Pad, a stationery shop, had cut the same almost-honey hair in a sharply wedged bob, and it had been years since anyone had seen her wearing anything besides a bikini or a linen shift. Vi, the youngest, was deeply tanned from surfing. She kept her hair short—less wind resistance, she claimed—trimming it above ears studded with tiny silver earrings.

Having quickly dispensed with her sandwich, Vi pushed aside the plate she hadn't bothered to use and said, "Okay. Now for the news. You two aren't going to believe this!"

"By the looks of the mailbag, you're about to get fired," Lily guessed in an awed voice, still gaping at the soda drips.

"Or get more demerits," agreed Pansy worriedly. "Did any of that soda actually make it to your mouth, Vi?"

"Not much," admitted Vi. "The second I opened the can, Garth Garrison's dog—you know, that chocolate Lab he named Gargantua?—well, he came after me like a hound from hell. I ran, of course."

"Very logical response," said Lily.

"I didn't want to use the Mace," Vi defended. "Not even Gargantua deserves that. Anyway, I accidently dumped the soda in the bag. But all is not lost." Grinning excitedly, Vi held up a cherry-stained envelope as her sisters looked on with dismayed expressions. The flap had come unglued, and in her effort to save the letter, Vi had slipped it from the envelope.

Pansy groaned. "You didn't read somebody's else's mail, did you?"

"I had to!" Vi protested. "I had no choice!"

"Violet Hanley!" Lily exclaimed in censure.

"Somebody on this island won the lottery," Vi blurted, untucking her uniform shirt and using it to dry the letter.

"The lottery?" echoed Pansy, thinking Seduction Island didn't have a lottery. "What lottery?"

"The New York lottery," Violet explained, her voice hitching. "Whoever it is won fifteen million dollars."

Pansy stared in shock. "Fifteen million dollars?" she echoed as if replacing the emphasis might make the words make better sense.

Violet nodded, stunned. "Yeah. Somebody on Seduction Island!"

Lily whistled. "And I thought we'd already had enough excitement for one week."

"You'd think," said Pansy, glancing through the screen door toward where a sliver of ocean was visible through the dunes. New York and local police were diving from an outboard motorboat, searching through the wreckage of a yacht that had exploded. Pansy had been thoroughly questioned, since she'd witnessed the fireworks, and then, less than an hour ago, she'd gotten another shock. A wooden plank had been salvaged from the wreck, and on it was the vessel's name, *Destiny*. It was the same name as the boat on which Jacques O'Lannaise had met Iris Hanley years ago. Pansy's heart clutched as she worried over the strange coincidence.

"Who won?" Lily asked impatiently.

"That's the thing," returned Violet. "I don't know. When I spilled the soda, the ink ran."

For a second, even fifteen million dollars didn't have the power to pull Pansy's attention to her sisters. Her gaze had shifted from the police and the *Destiny* to Castle O'Lannaise, the romantic white adobe estate perched on a bluff of the north shore, which could be seen from most points of the island. The property had changed hands countless times and had even been owned by a past president, but it was never inhabited long, which, for Pansy, only served to substantiate rumors that it was haunted by the dark, swarthy ghost of Jacques, whose star-crossed lover's past was so intimately tied to the Hanleys'.

Despite what finding a buyer for Castle O'Lannaise would mean for the realty business, Pansy loved the palatial estate, and for years she'd dreamed of finding a buyer who'd open it as a summer resort, just as Jacques O'Lannaise had planned. She'd felt that putting history to rest would restore Seduction Island's flagging economy, and she hoped the lottery winner would be interested in the estate.

"Garth Garrison was my next stop," Vi was saying. "Since the sorters put the letters in order, he's probably the winner." She groaned, thinking of the cranky horror novelist who lived in a tumbledown shack near the water. "I hate to think of him winning so much money," confessed Vi. "He's such a jerk."

"A good-looking jerk," reminded Lily.

"If you like the artistic type." Vi rolled her eyes as if to say she'd never registered that Garth was male. "Anyway, you all have to look at the address. See if you can read it. If it gets out that I ruined the mail again, I'll get fired."

Pansy sidled next to Lily. All three women stared at the business envelope. "That's definitely the lottery board's return address," Pansy murmured, shifting her gaze to forms the winner was supposed to fill out and sign. "And you can make out the word, 'Mr.'"

Lily grinned. "The winner's definitely male."

"Then he's married," said Vi. "He couldn't be single. We're not that lucky."

Summer storms aside, meeting so few eligible men was the one drawback to living on this otherwise idyllic island. Most men were salty retired sailors, and by the ripe old age of ten, the Hanleys had tired of having their hearts broken by seasonal tourists, whom they frequently vowed never to date, although they always did.

"Fifteen million," Pansy whispered, wondering if a buyer for Castle O'Lannaise was about to materialize.

"This is our zip code," offered Lily.

"What if Garth Garrison is the winner?" Vi said. "You know, Lily, you're right. He is kind of cute." Vi paused. "I mean, in a surly, self-absorbed, narcissistic sort of way."

Pansy frowned. "Did you ask him if he won?"

Vi gasped. "Are you kidding? He'd tear my head off if he knew I dripped cola into the mailbag. He's never forgiven me for that one manuscript of his I ruined. And it's not like he didn't have that book on disk. Besides which, who'd want to read something called *Bloodsuckers?*"

"You," Pansy told her.

Vi would prefer not to admit she was a secret admirer of Garth's lurid novels. "Well, anyway—" she huffed "—I didn't ask him. I bet he'd complain to Mr. Vincent, and I'd get fired."

"We'll send the letter back to the lottery board," decided Pansy reasonably. "They'll know how to redirect it."

Vi shook her head. "The letter's dated. If the winner doesn't get it in time, they'll lose the money."

Lily chewed her lower lip. "Could that really happen?"

"I don't know, but it would be terrible," Pansy agreed, knitting her brows. She'd hate for an accident such as this to cost a stranger the unbelievable sum of fifteen million dollars. "So much for 'Who Wants to be a Millionaire.'"

The Hanleys were die-hard fans of the show. "Hang it up, Regis," whispered Vi. "This guy's getting fifteen big ones."

"Maybe a tourist won," Lily speculated.

Pansy considered. "Nope. It's a local. Tourists never forward their mail. Usually someone at home picks it up while they're on vacation." She chuckled. "Besides, there're only two tourists." As a Realtor and part-time tour guide, she knew this was the worst rental season in history. And on Seduction Island, that was saying something.

"We have more than two," chided Lily.

"Three?" guessed Vi.

"Nearly five hundred," corrected Pansy. "But given our proximity to Nantucket and Martha's Vineyard..."

Vi raised a staying hand. "Please," she warned, "don't start talking about how this island's cursed, Pansy. Right now, I'm in real, ordinary, everyday trouble. I don't need to hear about your ghost pirate. C'mon. Does anybody have any bright ideas?"

"Lily," Pansy said, "you're on the town council and you're holding the summer meeting for visiting families tomorrow night. Half the locals come anyway, so we could announce this. We'll just say...that I found the letter."

"If no one claims it, we'll post it on one of the bulletin boards. At the grocery store or something," said Vi in relief. "Perfect. Can you believe someone on our island won fifteen million?"

The Hanleys, of course, knew Seduction Island was public and didn't really belong to them, but ever since Winston Hanley had arrived in the seventeen hundreds and built the house the women now shared, Hanleys had been taking responsibility for the island and its inhabitants. Besides, everybody knew the island hadn't become a city dweller's getaway, despite its proximity to New York City, because Jacques O'Lannaise cursed it when Iris Hanley hadn't married him years ago. After that, every Hanley had felt doubly responsible for whatever went wrong.

Lily gasped. "What if Lou Fairchild won?"

"Your fellow town councilman?" scoffed Vi. "You have no sense of irony, Lily. It has to be Garth Garrison. Someone as nice as Lou Fairchild would never win so much money."

"It's a shame Lou's not better looking," sighed Lily.

That was an understatement. Lou Fairchild, despite his name, had a face only a mother could love. But Pansy barely heard. Once more, she was imagining buying Castle O'Lannaise and turning it into the romantic resort it was meant to be. Suddenly, she glanced at her watch. "Oh, no! I've got to run," she said with a start, quickly rising and grabbing her jacket. "I'm meeting Ned Nelson."

"The guy renting Casa Eldora?" Lily asked, using the name of one of the rental cottages on the water.

"That's the one." Pansy had started hoping Ned would be as sexy as he sounded on the phone. Not that a mere man could compare with the fantasies she'd had about her favorite ghost, of course. Pausing at the door, Pansy traced her fingers over the screen, a slow smile tilting the corners of her mouth when she saw Castle O'Lannaise in the distance. "Whoever won the lottery is going to buy that castle," she announced, excited prickles of certainty washing over her skin.

"Well," returned Vi pragmatically, "maybe you can marry him and buy it yourself. But not if you bore him with tales about your mystery lover who haunts the dunes."

Lily mustered a fake French accent. "Jacques

O'Lannaise," she murmured, the name floating fluidly off her tongue.

"Don't you think it's odd the boat that exploded out there was called *Destiny?*" Pansy murmured.

"Explosions," Lily returned darkly. "A bad omen."

"I bet it was just a mechanical failure," said Vi, glancing toward the ocean.

Pansy's mind had filled with images of her ancestor, Iris Hanley, pacing the deck of a sailing ship, twirling a parasol on her shoulder, her long skirts swishing. According to family legend, she'd been sailing to distant cousins in New Orleans in hopes of meeting handsome suitors when pirates boarded the *Destiny*. Iris had trembled when one—a strapping man in tight breeches and a blousy white shirt with lace cuffs— stopped before her, his dark, unruly hair blowing wildly in the wind. But he didn't rob her. Instead the man sheathed his sword, wrapped his arms around Iris's waist and savaged her mouth, capturing her lips in a kiss like fire. A kiss that ruined Iris Hanley for marriage, since no other man's kiss ever surpassed it.

Twelve years later, in 1822, when a mysterious Frenchman arrived on the island to build Castle O'Lannaise, it was said he was that same pirate, that he'd arrived under an assumed name, made rich by the spoils of his plunder, to claim a woman he'd seen only once but whom he'd already branded with his fire.

"Pansy?"

Vi's voice startled her. "Huh?"

"Ned Nelson," Vi reminded.

"Right," Pansy whispered distractedly. Feeling whimsical as she pushed through the screen door, she fancied she wasn't going to Casa Eldora but into the dunes beside the cottage to meet her dark dream lover, Jacques O'Lannaise, and as her sandaled feet touched the sandy porch, she felt the coiled power in the hard body that held her, the brush of bristling black chest hair that erupted between the laces of his blouse and then the rush of blessed, fiery heat as Jacques's firm, wet mouth covered hers.

A second later, she found herself hoping—much more practically—that Ned Nelson would turn out to be cute.

2

"WELL, THAT'S the grand tour." Pansy turned a circle in Casa Eldora's living room, the low-slung heels of her white sandals tapping on the wide-planked wooden floor, her gaze taking in the serviceable plaid-upholstered furniture, then the ocean view through a picture window. "I'm sorry I forgot to turn on the AC when I dropped by earlier with the fruit basket," she apologized.

Rex shrugged. He'd already decided he liked Pansy Hanley just as she looked now, her damp skin glowing. She was even sexier than her husky voice had promised. Trouble was, Rex had gotten stuck in his Mr. Nice Guy tourist disguise, so Pansy wasn't impressed. In fact, when she'd first sized him up, he'd caught a look of downright disappointment. "Not to worry," Rex said. "The place'll cool off in a few minutes. And thanks for the tour." Pausing at the kitchen island, he opened a carton of lemonade, compliments of Hanley Realty. After pouring it over ice, he handed her a glass.

She took a grateful sip. "My pleasure, Mr. Nelson."

"Please—" Rex lifted his glass, glad for the feel of something cool. "Call me Ned."

"Ned," she repeated.

For a moment, they fell silent, two near strangers appreciating a view of the noontime sun, a brilliant white starburst perched high in a cerulean sky. Rex could almost see how it would look hours from now, dropping through vibrant strips of pink and lavender before ducking under the horizon, swallowed by the night. Cresting swells of green waves, the exact color of Pansy Hanley's eyes, were tumbling onto brown sand, the white, salty sea foam bubbling like boiling water before it was raked back, drawn to the sea with primal force, leaving broken shells, polished pebbles and scuttling hermit crabs. To his left, through a side window, Rex could see surreal dunes he was itching to explore.

She caught his gaze. "Those dunes are something, huh?"

He nodded. On much of the island, the sand swept into drifts near the shore, but the dunes near Casa Eldora rose to fifteen feet or more. "Looks like a moonscape," he commented.

"The area's restricted, since we want to preserve the dunes, but since most tourists are on the island's south side and locals rarely hang out here, you can walk in them if you're careful."

Rex chuckled. "You're suggesting I shouldn't wave at the cops before I venture in?"

She laughed. "I wouldn't. There's a hefty fine. But take it from a local. The area's not really patrolled. All we ask is that you not litter or disturb the sand. The restrictions are to keep kids out."

He smiled. "I shouldn't throw any wild parties, huh?"

"Not unless you invite me," Pansy quipped, thirstily taking another sip of lemonade. "Truly," she added. "You won't run into a soul."

"Then I'll definitely take a walk there."

"So, are you really satisfied with Casa Eldora?"

"It's perfect." Or it would have been if Rex was here on vacation. Or if he hadn't locked horns with Internal Affairs officer Judith Hunt as soon as he'd reached the island. He'd gone straight to the crime scene, hoping to hear news of his father, but Judith made it clear that Rex, the son of a suspect, was unwelcome, even threatening to prosecute if Rex involved himself in the investigation.

Rex had left the scene, changed into clothes he usually used for undercover work in New York, so he'd look like a tourist, then returned to shore where people were watching police dive into the wreckage. Introducing himself as Ned Nelson—a dopey, concerned tourist—Rex had questioned Judith. She'd never known it was Rex. He discovered Pansy Hanley witnessed the explosion, which meant he'd be spending more time with her, not that he wouldn't, anyway. He just wished he wasn't stuck in this ridiculous outfit for the duration of his stay. With any luck, he could risk taking it off every once in awhile, at least long enough to relieve his scalp, which was itching from the wig.

He sighed. During their tour, he'd asked what Pansy had seen, but hadn't gotten any more information than the police. Pansy had been awakened by a loud boom, but by the time she'd rushed to a window, only flames were visible. The sea extinguished them as the boat tilted and upended, jackknifing under water. The boat had only partially burned, so whoever was aboard had time to jump and had probably survived, but Pansy hadn't seen anyone make it ashore.

As with most eye witnesses, however, she'd probably seen more than she realized. It was Rex's job to probe her mind.

Probing her body would prove equally interesting. She'd removed her suit jacket, and the classy tank beneath—white against skin that was tanned nut brown—hugged high, firm breasts, exposing swells that quickened his pulse and tightened his groin.

He knew Pansy was feeling guilty since she'd forgotten to turn on the AC. She had bravely endured the heat, leaving Rex to appreciate how perspiration made the white silk of an otherwise unrevealing tank top cling, offering tantalizing glimpses of a lace bra and relaxed nipples beneath the fabric. Following her as she'd shown the house, Rex had found himself studying the nip of her waist, the flare of her hips and the swell of her backside. Seduction Island, indeed.

She was smiling. "I'm glad you like the place."

What he didn't like was being forced to meet Pansy Hanley while wearing an outfit specially devised by the NYPD to make him look like the perfect victim. He could easily see that the shaggy blond hair, puffed-out cheeks and black-framed glasses weren't impressing Pansy. But with Judith Hunt around, what choice did he have?

On the phone, Pansy's words had traveled on a sexy, throaty trill that should have prepared him for the overpowering physical response he was experiencing now. She had an open, direct manner, an easy smile and ironic humor, not to mention something of a whimsical air. Maybe that was due to her hair. Airy almost-honey layers swirled around her shoulders and face, framing sea-green eyes. Her face was round, her cheeks full and dimpled, and her bone structure seemed almost too delicate to carry off the female curves that were driving him wild. She was pursing her lips in a way he found oddly endearing.

"Lemonade too tart?" he guessed.

"Hanley Realty might find something sweeter," she admitted with a proprietal frown.

"Your company need look no further than its owner."

"Now that's sweet."

A five-year-old boy, not a grown man, could have paid the compliment, and every unseeing sweep of her gaze was starting to rankle. Yes, innocuous Ned Nelson, with his shaggy blond bangs that concealed a high, scholarly forehead and thick glasses that perched midway down his nose wasn't commanding much attention. Rex was sure she'd been disappointed when she saw him. Had she, too, fantasized about their meeting based on the easy telephone conversations they'd shared? Would she feel differently if baggy khaki pants weren't hiding Rex's hard muscles and sculpted contours? Or if the fastened top button of Rex's loose Hawaiian shirt wasn't covering a pelt of swirling jet hair?

He cursed his father and Judith Hunt for putting him in this position. If his father hadn't disappeared, Rex could have taken time off from policing, time he'd definitely like to spend getting to know Pansy. His gut instincts said Augustus had taken it upon himself to solve a crime. And if the Internal Affairs officer was more reasonable, she'd have shared information with Rex. He wouldn't have been forced to lower himself to subterfuge. Sighing, he sidled closer to Pansy, drawn by the soft parting of her lips and a whispery catch of breath that accelerated his heartbeat.

"You can see it from here," she murmured.

His eyes were studying the tilt of her nose and her wide, deep-set, sea-green eyes. "See what?"

"Castle O'Lannaise."

He looked to the distance where hot sun glanced off a dazzling white adobe compound. He couldn't make out all the structures, but a square, crenelated watchtower was visible, its arched cloisters leading onto iron-railed balconies.

"You can't tell from here, Ned," she explained, looking away from the estate long enough to capture Rex's gaze, "but Castle O'Lannaise was inspired by colonial Argentinian architecture. A square, columned walkway surrounds the main house, and the roofs are of red tile."

"Impressive."

She nodded. "Near the main house, there's an equestrian breeding lodge with a red brick floor and domed ceiling."

It was a long shot, but it took big money to buy such a place, so Rex started thinking of his father's ties to gangsters in Hell's Kitchen and Chinatown. Maybe the owner was someone Augustus had arrested in the past. Or maybe Castle O'Lannaise was otherwise connected to Augustus's disappearance. But how? "Who owns it?"

Pansy shrugged. "I'm not sure."

"Who's the Realtor?"

"Me. But the property's handled by a law firm, and it's been listed awhile. Various people have owned it over the years. Celebrities. Even a past president. An oil sheikh." Pansy sighed before pragmatically announcing, "It's haunted. That's why no one stays."

Despite her seriousness, Rex laughed. "Haunted?"

Tilting her chin and gazing at him from under lowered eyelids, she sent him what, in the old West, used to be called a thousand-yard stare. "You won't be laughing when you run into my ghost in the dunes," she warned archly.

He smiled playfully. "You really believe in ghosts?"

"This particular one? Absolutely."

He released another soft chuckle. "Why am I beginning to think there's a story in here somewhere?"

"Because there is." She paused a beat, building anticipatory tension. "The house was built by a Frenchman," she began. "Named Jacques O'Lannaise." When she chuckled, the sound was as delicate to Rex's ears as glass bells. "If that was his real name."

"The man happened to be in disguise, huh?" At least Rex had that much in common with the ghost of whom Pansy was so fond.

"It was rumored he was running from the law."

"A runner? I guess he was a jock as well as a Jacques."

Pansy giggled in spite of herself, then flatly said, "Mr. Nelson, that is the worst play on words I've ever heard."

He offered a look of mock concern. "You seem very attached to your ghost," he teased. "You seemed like such a nice woman, Pansy, but now I can see you're drawn to the criminal element."

A barely suppressed peal of laughter shook her shoulders. "Only in the case of Jacques O'Lannaise," she vowed solemnly.

"He must have been—" flicking his eyes over a face growing flushed with excitement, Rex had a sneaking suspicion that a few of Pansy's erotic fantasies had been inspired by Jacques "—quite something with the ladies."

"So they said," she murmured, her voice lapsing into dreamy cadences that lulled Rex like a ship on a rolling sea. "Right before the war of eighteen twelve a great-grandmother of ours—"

"Ours?" Rex interjected curiously.

"I was thinking of my two sisters, Lily and Violet."

Hanley sisters? This was getting more interesting by the minute. Apparently whimsy ran in the family. "You're all named after flowers?"

She nodded. "As was the ancestor I was about to mention."

Despite all the worry of the past few days, Rex was starting to enjoy himself. "Peony? Daisy? Poppy?"

"Iris," Pansy clarified. "In eighteen ten, Iris sailed from Seduction Island—then called Storm Island, by the way—to the city of New Orleans, where wealthy cousins waited to introduce her to Southern gentleman suitors."

"Because only crusty sailors inhabited Storm Island?" guessed Rex. "Ones with salty tongues who'd make better mates for serving wenches slinging ale in the local taverns?"

"Exactly." Pansy squinted playfully. "Are you sure you haven't taken one of the Hanley sisters' famous tours before?"

She'd mentioned she offered tours on Saturdays. "Never," he vowed.

He barely registered what she said next, only reacted to the magical, tinkling lilt of her voice. "The *Destiny*—that was Iris's ship—"

"Funny," he murmured. "That's the same name as the boat you saw explode."

Unfortunately, Pansy didn't want to explore the connection at the moment. "Yes," she continued. "It's an odd coincidence. Anyway, they'd almost reached New Orleans when pirates came aboard." Her voice lowered with a sense of impending threat. "They were after sugar cargo in the lower holds, of course, but they robbed the passengers, too."

Her lovely sea-green eyes had fixed once more in the distance, on Castle O'Lannaise, and Rex could tell history was coming alive in her imagination. He could taste salt on the air and feel the sea breeze on his cheeks and hear the rustle of the ladies' long skirts and lace petticoats. "And?" he prompted.

"Well—" Pansy's voice sharpened, taking on a strangely rehearsed quality that, despite the dreamy tone, told Rex she'd honed this story over many retellings. "One pirate, in particular, took a liking to Iris. Now," she paused, "you have to imagine this fellow."

"Do I?" murmured Rex.

"Yes. He was tall, over six feet, and wearing tight black breeches, black boots and a loose white shirt with ruffled cuffs that was laced by crisscrossed leather. A belt circled his waist, and a long, weathered leather sheath hung from it. Sunlight glinted on the sharp silver blade of his sword, temporarily blinding Iris as he thrust it into the sheath."

"Very dramatic," Rex assured.

Turning her head slightly, Pansy leveled Rex with a

stare. "Iris squinted," she continued. "Which is why she didn't see it coming."

Sucked in by the story, Rex murmured, "See what coming?"

A slow smile stretched Pansy's lips. "The kiss."

Talking about kisses with Pansy was more unsettling than it should have been, and Rex tried to look less curious than he was. "This pirate, this stranger—he kissed Iris?"

Pansy's cheeks flushed with such deep color that she, not Iris, could have been the recipient of the man's bold move. "He stepped right up to her, wrapped his arms around her waist, hauled her to him and kissed her soundly."

Clearly, Pansy had imagined all this in great detail. If Iris had looked anything like Pansy, Rex thought, he thoroughly understood the piratical impulse. "Go on."

"Later," she continued, her tone conspiratorial, "it was rumored that the pirate was a brother of Jean and Pierre Lafitte, and that he came North in eighteen twenty when his brothers fled to Mexico."

"The plot thickens."

"Well, keep in mind," Pansy warned, "that the people who witnessed that kiss said it went on forever. It was so unusual that it ruined Iris for the suitors she was supposed to meet in New Orleans, and the cousins had to send her back to Storm Island unmarried. After that—" Pansy shook her head in censure. "Iris," she clarified, "wouldn't even go on any more dates."

"And Storm Island was renamed Seduction Island?"

"Correct."

Rex had become thoroughly mesmerized by the way Pansy's mouth moved. Up, down. Back, forth. Puckered, slack. Any way he looked at it, he wanted to feel it on his. "Must have been some kiss."

"Even after Iris returned home," emphasized Pansy, "she continued turning men down."

"Given that they kept trying, she must have been beautiful."

"She was."

"Runs in the family."

"Thanks," she said distractedly, her eyes on Castle O'Lannaise. Rex sighed again, cursing the moment he'd worn clothes intentionally calculated to undercut his male prowess. Pansy hadn't even registered Rex was a man, not a mistake she'd make if he was shirtless, wigless and wearing jeans. "So, what happened?"

"Years passed. And then a mysterious Frenchman arrived and built Castle O'Lannaise. He meant to open it as a resort, catering to the wealthy. Just a month before he did, he tried to claim Iris. Her father correctly suspected this was the pirate who'd kissed her aboard the *Destiny*, a man made rich by the ill-gotten spoils of war, and so Iris was forbidden to see Jacques, despite the fact that her marriage prospects were dim."

"Dim?"

"By this time, she was twenty-seven."

"Ancient," Rex commiserated. The rapture on Pansy's face was warming his blood, as was the naked desire in her eyes. No doubt about it, Pansy dreamed of being kissed with a passion capable of ruining her for all other men. In fact, if the hunger in those sea-green eyes was any indication, she craved more than a mere kiss. Rex found himself wondering just how many lovers she'd had. "Surely people so...so aroused by each other had to meet eventually, didn't they, Pansy?"

"In the dunes," she returned, her eyes glazed. "They wrote to each other, too. We still have their letters."

"They survived all these years?"

She shrugged. "We Hanleys preserve our heritage."

Intrigued, Rex visualized heavy cream paper and calligraphic letters written with a quilled pen. What would two people so in love say to each other? "Do Hanleys let outsiders read them?"

Looking as if she'd just come back to earth, Pansy laughed softly, her eyes glinting flirtatiously. "Sometimes."

"What's the price of admission?"

When she paused, he wondered if she was thinking of that kiss like fire again. "I'll be happy to let you see them."

He figured there wasn't much hope in arranging a tryst of their own, not while he was in this getup. She was obviously interested in him, but only as a friend. "So, how does the story end?"

"Badly, I'm afraid." Pansy's lips pursed grimly. "That summer, just as a storm hit, Jacques O'Lannaise was waiting for an answer to his marriage proposal. You have to understand that he was a man out of his element. He was far from New Orleans, farther still from his native France. He'd never really wanted to be a pirate anyway, but he'd done whatever was necessary to survive. Until the day he saw Iris."

"Ah. Love changed him?"

"Completely. For hours, he stood in the watchtower, a wild wind blowing around him, hoping to see Iris riding her mare through the dunes. He didn't know her father had evacuated the family, hoping to reach the mainland. The letter of explanation she wrote never reached him. We still have it today."

"But when the family got back..."

Pansy shook her head, sadness coming into her eyes. "They were swept out to sea."

Hardly the happy ending Rex expected. "She died?"

"Jacques never opened the resort. From the watchtower, he cursed this island, and ever since, we've been hit by the worst storms in this part of the Atlantic. It's so bad we rarely get many tourists."

"So, Jacques O'Lannaise still haunts the dunes, hoping Iris will return?"

"Yep." Tucking her chin, she surveyed him from under half-lidded eyes, and Rex reminded himself she'd been feeding him standard tourist fare. This was probably what she said, verbatim, on Saturday tours. No doubt, she mesmerized guests. She said, "I guess every town in America has a resident ghost."

But not every ghost was loved by a woman as tantalizing as Pansy. She'd caught Rex in her spell, weaving a story of love, loss and mysticism he was powerless to resist.

Her throaty voice sounded ripe for seduction. "So, if you meet a dark, swarthy man in the dunes, or see shadows in the windows of Castle O'Lannaise, you'll know who it is."

Rex lowered his voice and asked in the same seductive tone, "Have you seen him, personally?"

"I'll never tell." Her smile deepened. "You'll have to join one of our tours. Vi books guests, Lily drives the bus and I give the spiel about the island's history."

"You do a good job." Before this moment, hardened cop Rex Steele had never imagined he could be jealous of a ghost.

"We depart from the south dock every two hours on Saturdays, beginning at eight a.m."

"It's not a full-time business?"

She shook her head regretfully. "I wish. But there are too many storms here. Not enough tourists."

In a flash fantasy, he imagined himself taking the tour twice—once as innocuous Ned Nelson and then as dark, swarthy Rex Steele, who he suspected might bear a passing resemblance to Jacques O'Lannaise. Rex was raven-haired, anyway. "I'll be sure to sign up at some point."

"It's so hot," she apologized once more, changing the subject. "I'm really sorry I forgot to turn on the AC."

He pressed his ice-chilled glass to her bare arm. Offering an enticing shiver, she said, "Thanks."

Thank you, he thought, noticing how her nipples beaded against the white top. She didn't even register the effect on him. He grimaced. Why would a woman worry about how effeminate, sensitive Ned Nelson would react to her arousal? Hell, Pansy probably figured she could strut around Casa Eldora stark naked without bringing out the animal in Ned.

She was wrong. Rex was far too aware of her. And of the couch not two feet away. He imagined stripping off her clothes, setting her on the cushions, thrusting inside her. Her scent, stirred by stifling summer heat, stole his breath and filled the room. His groin suddenly ached, pulling with pangs of want.

All the while, Rex didn't register on her radar. By wearing the costume calculated to throw Judith Hunt off the scent, he'd become the exact opposite of Pansy's dream lover. While she stared into the distance, oblivious, he was imagining making love to her again, this time hard and fast on the sand of the dunes. Maybe he'd drag her into the wild surf, letting the hot waves drench her.

He wondered what she'd look like in a bikini.

Then a wet white bikini.

Then naked.

Somehow, he already knew how the slow slide of his hands on her thighs would feel, how touches of her breath would stir hairs at his nape, how he'd burn with need for her.

She glanced at her watch. "Well, it's been nice to meet you, Ned, but I'd really better go. Oh," she added in afterthought, "speaking of summer storms. Tomorrow night there's a town meeting. My sister Lily's on the council with a man named Lou Fairchild. Once a week, they go over safety precautions for guests. You know...how to stay out of the undertow. Evacuation procedures in case of storms. We suggest that everyone come."

"Storms, evacuations," he teased. "You sure know how to show a guy a good time."

"You'd be surprised," she quipped.

"I like surprises."

She merely smiled, not nearly as affected by the flirtation as he would have liked. "We've found a damaged letter from the New York lottery board, and since we can't make out who it's addressed to, we'll be asking someone to claim it. Someone on the island won fifteen million dollars, so it'll be interesting to see who."

Rex tried not to react, knowing it was for him. "The letter was damaged?"

Her eyes sparkled with humor as she sized up Rex, then decided to share. "The truth is, my sister Vi's a mail carrier, and she spilled a soda into the mailbag. She can be a bit of a klutz, and we're afraid if she ruins anymore mail, she'll be fired. So we're going to pretend I found the letter."

Looking at her, Rex found himself thinking of her fantasy life again, one in which he suspected she allowed herself to be plundered by a pirate. Then he wondered how he was going to claim the letter without alerting Judith Hunt to the fact he'd remained on the island. If he claimed the letter as Ned Nelson, that would also bring unwanted attention his way. He'd prefer to retrieve the letter anonymously.

Pansy was frowning. "There were forms from the lottery board for the winner to fill out."

"What if no one claims it?"

"We'll post it."

That was a relief. "Where?"

"The grocery store or the post office. We'll announce the location at the meeting. Can you imagine that much money?"

Unfortunately, yes. When he thought of what his father had supposedly stolen, Rex hardly wanted to. And when he thought of the lottery, unexpected anger burrowed under his skin, especially when Pansy's eyes returned to Castle O'Lannaise. He hated to think money could buy a woman's happiness, but there was no doubt Pansy was in love with the castle and Jacques O'Lannaise. For a brief second, he felt jealous. But that was crazy! Was he really threatened by a man who didn't even exist? A ghost who haunted an old equestrian estate? "Ah," he suddenly guessed. "You're hoping to find a buyer for your castle, aren't you?"

Color rose on her cheeks. "Am I so transparent?"

"Maybe," he admitted. With one look, Rex felt he'd known her for years. Even more, she'd unwittingly challenged him to give her what she most craved—a castle. Or better yet, a kiss of fire. She was so...original. So unlike city women. Her island paradise was completely different from Manhattan, the only home he'd ever known. He thought of summers there, the baking heat on the sidewalks, the short tempers, the power outages. He was always glad to escape. Could Pansy be the woman he'd fantasized meeting year after year?

Coming back to the issue at hand, he decided Judith Hunt probably wouldn't attend the council meeting. He'd go and at least find out where the Hanleys meant to post the letter. Preoccupied, he barely noticed Pansy had left his side and set her glass down. She was leafing through some sketches in a portfolio beside the couch.

"These are beautiful," she murmured.

Something fierce and protective kicked in when Rex realized what she was doing, and he braced himself for criticism, but Pansy only continued going through the landscape drawings from his last vacation. Somewhere in the far reaches of his mind, he could hear his father saying, "Punch me again. You've got to prove you're a man. You keep drawing pictures and the boys downtown are gonna call you a sissy."

She said, "You're good."

Easy laughter masked his watchfulness. "Tour guide, Realtor, art critic...what next?"

"Most people in my family draw," Pansy explained, glancing through the window at the beach. "It comes with growing up on an island, I guess. People get bored. Iris even sketched Jacques O'Lannaise."

"Ah. So, you know what your pirate looks like."

Color stained her cheeks. "He's not my pirate," she defended.

Rex grinned. "Are you sure?"

Her chuckle floated into his blood. "I admit," she countered, "Jacques has captured my imagination for years."

"Pansy," Rex returned, "you're a fascinating woman."

He wished more than the light of new friendship was sparking in her eyes. She shrugged. "I've had a few fantasies about this pirate, okay? Just don't tell anyone."

He held out a hand, and they shook on it. Her touch sent tingles up his arm. "Your secret's safe with me."

She surveyed him. "Do you have any secrets?"

Innocuous Ned Nelson? He laughed. "Are you kidding?"

She grinned. "I guess you wouldn't," she said, reacting to his honest looks and turning back to the drawings. "So I'll just have to trust you to keep mine. They're good," she offered again. "You're..."

The lie he'd told Judith Hunt rolled easily from his tongue. "An architect."

"From talking to you on the phone, I should have guessed it was something artistic. That explains the drawing skills. And you like to read, too." She lifted a book. "Poetry?"

He ignored the urge to defend himself, but she was looking at him as if he was a highly unusual male specimen. Why couldn't men enjoy poetry without feeling like effete intellectuals? Rex wanted to let her in—more than he ever had anyone at first meeting—but he didn't like exposing a self he usually kept from prying eyes, except on these month-long summer sojourns. "Yeah," he finally said, "I like poetry."

"Me, too."

Surprisingly, another few moments of conversation passed, during which they traded favorite authors. Then she said, "If you like poetry, you really might appreciate Iris's letters." She paused. "Most men don't. Like poetry, I mean."

There it was again. Most men. Once more, he was conscious of being in the wig, the oversize clothes, with his damn cheeks puffed out and a ridiculous pair of glasses sliding down his nose. His father's rough voice ghosted through his mind. *Harder, Rex. You've got to pound the other guy, let him know you're a man.* "What do most men like?" he taunted softly. "Guzzling beer and belching while rooting for sports teams?"

Looking genuinely delighted, she laughed. "No brothers, so I really couldn't say."

His eyes narrowed, and his voice turned husky. "What about lovers?"

Surprised, she quickly recovered. "Only Jacques O'Lannaise," she quipped, and from the guilty light of pleasure in her eyes, Rex couldn't help but surmise how satisfying the fantasies had been for her. After a moment, she amended her words, saying she'd had some long-term boyfriends but no one serious. When she glanced at her watch again, Rex had the sudden, primal urge to haul her off her feet and drag her to a bedroom, a place where he damn well knew he excelled. "Sorry," she murmured. "I'd better go."

Stay. "I'll walk you to your car."

His eyes were hot on hers as he placed a hand beneath her elbow, lifted her jacket from a wall peg and guided her to the door. The room had cooled, and as they stepped into a rippling wave of heat, she reacted once more, her shiver making him imagine it coming on a sigh of pleasure.

"Don't forget to come to the town meeting, Ned," she said when they reached her black compact car.

She smiled as he opened a door that had absorbed heat like a conductor. As she got in, her hem rose, and his breathing shallowed at the flash of a bare, slender, long-boned thigh. "You could fry eggs on the car," he said.

"Trying to get a breakfast invitation?"

He laughed. "Am I so transparent?" he asked, echoing her earlier words. Before she could answer, he said, "If I don't see you at the town meeting, we'll hook up at the bonfire afterward, Pansy."

He closed the door, and as she started the car, she powered down the window. "I could show you the inside of Castle O'Lannaise," she offered. "It's not on our tour. It's got a locked gate, but I can let you in."

"I'll need you along," he said, "to protect me from your ghost. If he sees you with another man, he might get jealous."

She smiled. "Of course."

"And Iris's letters," he reminded.

"It's not just a bonfire," she returned, a barely noticeable hitch in her voice. "There's a dance on the beach with music. We have one every week. My sisters and I always go. I'll know more about my schedule then. We'll arrange a time for you to read the letters."

He tried to ignore the friendly warmth of her gaze, a warmth that couldn't begin to answer the hotter, darker things she'd been inspiring since she walked into Casa Eldora. The edgy eroticism, wrought by her unconscious challenge to his masculinity, was the worst. He was definitely a man, and he'd like nothing more than to apprise Pansy Hanley of that fact. As far as he was concerned, she was lucky to get out of here with her clothes on. He said, "I'll enjoy seeing you again." What an understatement.

Moments later, he was still standing on the shell driveway, watching the car round a last bend in the dunes where Pansy's French pirate lover supposedly walked at night. Inhaling deeply, Rex was imagining a kiss of fire. It wouldn't be the first time he'd simultaneously solved a crime and pursued a romance. He'd never been given to mild flirtation, though. He was drawn to women with whom he could envision a future, and he could definitely see himself living in an island paradise with a woman who possessed sensitivity and a love of poetry, not to mention the capacity to arouse him to distraction. Already, he could feel the scalding heat of her mouth, the tingling of her lips, the dark thrill that would race through his blood when he claimed her. And Rex would claim her soon.

3

"USUALLY, we have two or three severe storms per summer. They come quickly, without warning," Pansy was saying into a microphone. She chuckled. "That's why this was called Storm Island in the seventeen hundreds. Now, some of you, I know, have taken our bus tour of the island, so you've heard the story. During a particularly bad storm, a woman named Iris Hanley was parted from her seductive husband-to-be, a man who later walked the dunes at night, wishing for her return. That's why the island came to be called Seduction Island.

"It was also sometimes said that the man, Jacques O'Lannaise, cursed this island when he found out his lover was lost at sea, which is why we began having even more storms in the next century. So, as you can see, the island has remained true to its earlier name."

"What should we do if there's a storm?" called someone from the audience.

"Good question. Often people in rental cottages elect to help board windows or sandbag before an evacuation. The storms rarely last long, and if you're forced to leave, chances are you'll be back in your vacation home within two days. It's a good idea to keep extra water on hand. If you decide to wait out the storm instead of leaving the island, supplies could run low."

Rex, who'd slipped in through a back door, half listened as he scanned the crowded town hall, one of many buildings lining Sand Road, only a few minutes walk from Casa Eldora. With the star-studded skies so clear, it was hard to imagine impending storms, but the place was packed, with people seated on bleachers or in gray metal folding chairs. Up front, Pansy was standing behind a podium. Two women who bore a physical resemblance, presumably her sisters, were seated beside her, as was a man, probably the town council member Pansy had mentioned, Lou Fairchild. Rex's lips tilted into a smile at the irony of the man's name. Hardly a fair child, at least not physically, Lou was huge, with pockmarked cheeks and a hooked nose that made his constant, good-natured grin seem a little ghoulish. He also seemed like a genuinely nice guy.

Pansy's lilting voice had captured the crowd, and she looked even prettier than Rex remembered, wearing a sleeveless, lime-green blouse and wraparound skirt printed with interlaced jewel-colored diamonds. Watching her, Rex was reminded of how, after their last meeting, he'd stripped off the wig, glasses and cheek pads and wandered barefoot through the dunes at nightfall, half hoping she'd appear. If Pansy saw him without the disguise, would he reveal his identity, trusting her not to tell Judith he was still in town? Or would he pretend to be a stranger? Maybe make up another name? A smile lifted his lips. Would he pretend to be the ghost of Jacques O'Lannaise? He'd seriously considered such a plan as he'd watched her leave Casa Eldora.

A wistful sigh rumbling in his chest, Rex had

wished he could talk to Pansy before the bonfire dance, but the cumbersome costume had started bothering him again—glue in the wig was causing a rash on his scalp, the cheek pads kept drying his mouth, and the glasses were pinching his nose. He'd removed the items before taking a nap, only to wake and realize he was late for the meeting. Because of the announcement about the lottery letter, he had to be here. As soon as the meeting was over, he'd change into the Ned Nelson getup and meet Pansy as planned.

He was hoping she hadn't announced where the letter would be posted when he realized Judith Hunt was seated near the front, banked by officers. *Great.* Rex couldn't leave until he figured out how to get his hands on the letter, but sans the wig, cheek pads, glasses and loose clothes, Judith would recognize him, and he'd told her he was leaving the island.

Fortunately, vacationing couples and families formed a buffer between him and Judith, and the only person who really seemed to notice him was a tanned boy of about six, who wrenched in his chair and stared curiously. The kid was shirtless, his bony rib cage exposed, and damp swim trunks ending at knobby knees clung to him. Freckles were scattered over pink cheeks, and although it was dark outside, the boy's nose was splotched with white sunblock. When he grinned and waved, Rex had to fight not to laugh. The kid's front teeth were missing.

Rex waved gamely back.

As the kid whirled around, unexpected emotion twisted inside Rex. The kid, seated so happily between an indulgent mom and dad, seemed to represent the life Rex could have lived—if he hadn't been born Rex Steele. While he was growing up, no one had asked if he wanted to be a cop, only which badge and division. "What do ya say, Rex?" his father would ask, playfully clapping his shoulder. "You want to work at Midtown? Manhattan South? What about the thirteenth precinct?" Or, "What's it gonna be? The SWAT team? A Mountie? Maybe detective for you?"

The kid waved again.

Rex winked.

Years ago, he'd vowed never to put a kid through the daily worry he'd felt growing up. A kid needed to feel sure his dad would make it home for dinner. But Rex was thirty-four, and more and more often, during his month-long summer sojourns, he found himself wondering why he'd remained a cop. Wouldn't he rather have another lifestyle? A wife? A kid like the one who was grinning at him?

The deal with his mother was pressuring him, too. While he doubted she'd give her lottery winnings to the Galapagos Islands if he, Truman and Sully didn't marry, Rex knew she was right. They needed partners. Being alone wasn't good for a man. Often, Rex wished he knew how to do something other than police work, since he'd never willingly expose a family to the dangers of his profession. But if he found a woman now, he'd wind up with five million dollars—more money than he could even comprehend, more than enough to start over.

Was that why Pansy was so intriguing? If he was rich, what was to stop him from keeping busy by doing unskilled work and learning to paint pictures? Surely a lot of women would prefer a ne'er-do-well painter to a man who could get killed in the line of duty, wouldn't they? Despite the lack of support for his favorite endeavors from most of his family, wasn't it his responsibility—his alone—to give up being a cop and explore his dreams? Hell, wasn't that something he should have done a long time ago? He'd lived the life of a hero, but wasn't it more heroic to follow your heart?

Sighing as he pushed aside the questions, Rex hoped once more that Judith wouldn't notice him. All day, he'd combed the beach for evidence that his father had come ashore. He'd found none, but without Judith seeing him, he'd bagged some area samples in case he, Truman and Sully needed them later. He hated to think it, but if the worst thing happened, if his father's body was found elsewhere, trace evidence might prove he'd been on the island and for how long.

"Thank you for giving me your kind attention," Pansy was saying. "Now, before we all head out for the bonfire dance on the south shore, I'm going to hand things over to Lily Hanley and Lou Fairchild again. These two natives will be giving you more helpful hints about keeping your family safe."

Pansy stepped from the microphone, then leaned toward it once more, adding, "Oh, I almost forgot! Earlier, we announced we found a letter from the New York lottery board, addressed to a winner on the island. Apparently, fifteen million dollars went to this lucky person a few weeks ago! Since no one's claimed the letter, it's been posted a few doors down, on the bulletin board at Zaw's Grocery. Please," Pansy added, "if you've come in late and know you've won the New York lottery, you need to pick up the letter...."

Her voice trailed off when her eyes found his. A
beat passed. Then another. Rex tried to look away, but
those sea-green eyes captured his and wouldn't let go.
Everyone else in the audience became a blur. Some
turned in their seats, sensing the thread of connection
between Pansy and Rex. It was electric, uncanny. He
felt as if he'd been asleep for a long time and had suddenly startled awake. For a second, he actually forgot
he wasn't wearing the disguise. He assumed she recognized him, and he started to wave—until he remembered that his dark, tousled hair hung free, waving over his ears. He was wearing stylishly baggy
black jeans, a button-down shirt that stuck to his skin
in the heat and thick-soled earth sandals.

He should have looked like a stranger. But Pansy
was staring as if she knew him. Was she the first person to ever see through his disguise? Doubtful, he decided. But her eyes were wide open. Rex was riveted
to the spot. Why was she staring so hard? Was it attraction to a stranger? Or did she sense a similarity between him and the man she knew as Ned Nelson? Rex
wished there was time to find out, but it was only a
matter of seconds before Judith followed Pansy's
gaze, glanced over her shoulder like so many of the
tourists and discovered his presence.

Judith would identify him immediately. Not as Ned
Nelson, but as a seasoned cop honing in on her investigation, trying to clear his father's name. Even worse,
Judith had threatened to prosecute if she caught Rex
on the island. Still drawn by the stark interest in
Pansy's eyes, Rex wished he could go to her, but he
knew he couldn't. Cursing inwardly, he turned before

Judith saw him and slipped through the door, vanishing into the hot, velvet night.

JACQUES O'LANNAISE? Oh, my God, it was him! Pansy's heart was in her throat as she edged farther from the microphone, mumbling excuses to Vi and Lily, saying she had to get to a ladies' room. Or maybe she should just sit down. Blood was rushing through her veins, making her dizzy. For the heart-stopping second before the stranger vanished, she couldn't blink. And then she didn't want to. What if her vision of the perfect male vanished?

Don't go! she urged.

But he'd already edged backward through the door. He was gone! Strange magic had breathed life into the penciled sketches drawn by Iris Hanley so many years ago. It was as if Jacques had been reincarnated! Just as in his pictures, the man had been tall, well muscled and hollow-cheeked, his face just shy of gaunt and coated by dark stubble.

But surely she was mistaken! Surely he was just another vacationer! She'd waited, hoping he'd suddenly speak, calling out a question in a squeaky voice. Or maybe, if she caught up to him, his Adam's apple would bob—something, anything to dispel this sense of magic and make him seem human. He couldn't be a ghost! Ghosts were...transparent. The closing door would have moved right through him. But he'd looked like a solid sheet of rock-hard male muscle.

She was losing her mind! Had her deepest erotic fantasies run so wild that she'd conjured Jacques O'Lannaise from thin air? She shook her head to clear it of confusion. As creatively flighty as she was, if only when it came to Jacques O'Lannaise, she didn't believe that! Maybe it was because Ned Nelson, whom she'd met today, had been so, well, nice. After their easy phone conversations, she'd felt so hopeful. Deep down, she'd teased herself, fantasizing that Ned would arrive on the island, looking like her dream lover, his dark eyes flashing with awareness and sexual promise.

Of course he'd turned out to be quite the opposite in both appearance and demeanor. Mumbling another excuse and feeling glad Lou Fairchild had taken the microphone, Pansy left the front of the auditorium and made her way down a side aisle. When she reached the back, she stepped outside and looked right, then left. He'd vanished!

Her hungry eyes searched Sand Road, but it was deserted. Where could he have gone? Had he really vanished? Had he been a figment of her imagination?

Damn, she thought as she headed uncertainly down the sidewalk. If she asked Vi and Lily if they'd seen him, they'd think she was crazy. "So, just keep looking," she muttered. Yes, she'd see him any second now—and realize he didn't really look like Jacques!

Drawing a sharp breath, she ducked into a shady recess in front of the Island Bank. *What am I doing?* she wondered, knowing as she sank against the plate glass that she'd have to follow if she saw him again. Ever since childhood, when she'd heard of Jacques O'Lannaise, the pirate who'd ravished Iris had played heavily in her fantasy life, and this man looked so much like him.

What if he was Jacques O'Lannaise? What if the ghost was seeking her out since she resembled her ancestor, Iris? Pansy pushed aside the insanely romantic thought. No, he was a real man. One who just happened to look like her dream lover. He was compelling, too, his pull as overwhelming as a magnet's, stronger than the tides. There! Relief flooded her as he appeared on the sidewalk, coming from a newsstand. Clearly, he was no phantom. Not unless ghosts window-shopped and were as solid as walls.

Seaweed and fish smells undulated on the salt breeze, and the breath in her lungs felt steamy. It would be cooler in the shadowy dunes, near the water. Closer to the buildings, it was hot. Gritty sand blew across the paved road, sprinkling her skin. Although the sun had long ago dropped over the horizon, the sidewalk was baking, softening the rubber soles of her sandals.

She watched as he turned, glancing over a shoulder. Sleek black hair was pushed back from a high forehead that made him look forbiddingly intelligent. His self-possession affected her most. She saw his attentive eyes search the street, as if he suspected she was following him.

"The guy's just a tourist," she assured herself, but even as she spoke, she felt sure the words were a lie. Something—maybe the romance of the dark velvet night or the magic of the moon and stars—was convincing her that this stranger was the man of her dreams. Quite literally.

"The guy's probably looking for someplace that's open so he can buy shells," she said nervously. She wasn't exactly sure she wanted to meet a ghost—if he was a ghost. "Which, of course, he isn't," she muttered. She listened to the breakers crashing on the nearby beach, and as the sea breeze blew strands of hair across her cheeks, it brought the taste of salt to her lips...a taste that could have been the stranger's bare skin. Just as she sighed, sinking against the sun-warmed concrete side of a building, she realized the stranger was starting to head for the dunes.

Pansy startled. What had she been expecting? That he'd fade in a ghostly manner, becoming insubstantial by slow degrees? That he'd become transparent as he entered the dunes, so that she could see straight through him?

"Go back inside," she urged, but as she edged from hiding, she was powerless but to follow wherever he led and take this adventure to its climax. Who was he? And where...

Zaw's?

No, it couldn't be! Her heart was pounding, her throat burning. Adrenaline was pulsing through her veins as he pushed through the first of two glass doors. Rather than enter the store, he paused in the glassed-in foyer and studied the bulletin board. As he stood under bright, fluorescent lights, he looked real enough. He definitely wasn't a ghost. He wasn't a local, either. Pansy knew every living soul on the island. He was a tourist, popping into Zaw's for milk and eggs on his way back to a cottage he rented from another Realtor.

If she didn't find out who he was tonight, she'd make a few simple phone calls tomorrow. Easy enough. As good-looking as he was, the island's other Realtors—all women—would remember his name and which cottage he'd rented.

Her jaw slackened. "The lottery letter?"

The man was scanning ads for used furniture, crab traps and fish bait, and he eased a scrap of paper from beneath a pushpin. Was it the lottery letter? Or had he taken something else from the board? A reward announcement for a lost animal? An ad for a sand blower? Whatever it was, he folded and shoved it into his back pocket, then he exited Zaw's, heading for the lower end of Sand Road and Ned Nelson's place. But why would he be going toward Casa Eldora?

Without missing a step, he leaned with lithe, almost predatory agility, slipped off his sandals, then hooked his fingers through the toeholds, letting the sandals dangle. Didn't the sidewalk burn his feet? she wondered, then gasped as he continued undressing, single-handedly unbuttoning his shirt. Tearing her eyes from him, she ducked inside Zaw's.

She was trying to keep her mind on the lottery, but instead she was imagining jet silk hair tangling on his bare chest. She felt as if she already knew the muscles, how they'd glide beneath her hands—smooth, polished and hard, like sun-warmed marble. Was the mysterious stranger who bore such a striking resemblance to Jacques O'Lannaise really the lottery winner?

Excitement gushed through her. She felt so hot she barely registered the icy blast of Zaw's air conditioner. She'd never done anything like this before! She felt...naughty! But she'd been right! She'd pinned the letter between an ad for Louise McDermit's cat Millie's kittens and one for Kirk Kilby's twin engine outboard—and it was gone! Could she catch up with the man? Meet him? Talk him into buying Castle O'Lannaise? She chuckled, feeling swept off her feet, wildly giddy. Lily had convinced herself that Lou Fairchild had won, just as Vi kept supposing the winner was Garth Garrison. But only Pansy knew the truth, that he was a tall, dark, sexy stranger.

Pushing through the glass doors, she stepped into a wave of rippling heat. He was crossing Sand Road! If she didn't hurry, she'd lose him! Maybe she'd never see him again! She had to find out where he was staying, at least. Jogging, she crossed the road, and when she felt the warm, grainy sand gush into her sandals, she slipped them off.

He was vanishing into the dunes! Should she call out? Would he respond? High sand walls buffered the roar of nearby surf as she followed him into the sand drifts, her heart clutching when she saw he'd left no prints. Was he really a ghost? "The wind," she whispered. "It's blowing the sand, that's all. Perfectly reasonable." And anyway, she saw something that could have been footprints, didn't she? Or were they animal tracks?

Even her lifetime acquaintance with the dunes couldn't mitigate their power tonight. A moonscape, Ned Nelson had called it, and he was right. Lit by the yellow light of a three-quarter moon, the majestic sweep of the drifts cast long, dark shadows, then peaked in bluffs fifteen feet high. They curled, swooping downward, creating the valleys where she and the stranger walked. She was about to climb to the top of a bluff so she could gauge her direction when a sliver of sea glistened through the sandy maze, and she saw a stretch of beach near Casa Eldora.

Ned Nelson's cottage was dark, the beach deserted. Far down the shoreline, she could see the anchored boat from which the police had been diving, but they were gone for the night. "The *Destiny*," she whispered. Was it really coincidence that a ship of that name had mysteriously exploded here? It seemed crazy. But what if Jacques's curse on the island had caused the wreck? After all, Jacques had first kissed the lady he'd lost on another boat named *Destiny*.

When she saw the stranger near the water, Pansy shrank behind a soft swell of sand. "Oh, yeah," she whispered, her heart skipping a beat. "Right about now, this guy definitely looks real."

Powerful shoulders were shrugging from the shirt. Shaking it like a blanket, he set it on the ground, weighing it down with his sandals so the wind wouldn't carry it away. His moon-touched belly was rock-hard and the ridge of ribs enticing, but time stopped when he casually rested a hand on the belt-less waistband of his jeans. Pansy's belly clutched against the sudden heat pooling there. Her body tightened. Inside, she melted. She told herself to turn around and leave, but she wanted to...see the rest of him. Every inch.

Her tongue licked dry lips as, one by one, with excruciatingly slow flicks of his wrist, he popped open the buttons to his jeans, his hand gilding down a denim fly that gloved an unmistakable male bulge. He looked so full there, so heavy. The V widened as denim parted. White flashed—skin or briefs, she didn't know. She couldn't move. Or breathe. She was frozen in place. Her throat ached. Her body trembled with the need to see more. Her fingers itched to touch.

What the hell was she doing? she wondered vaguely. But surely she wasn't the only woman bold enough to watch an unspeakably handsome man undress on a public beach if given the opportunity, right? And he had fifteen million dollars! Pansy couldn't believe it. This astonishingly gorgeous man could buy Castle O'Lannaise! He could make her dreams come true! Surely, once it was opened as the resort Jacques had planned before Iris died, Jacques's ghost would be put to rest. If his curse on the island really was responsible for the unusual number of storms, wouldn't they cease? Would the tourist industry be revived on Seduction Island?

You're definitely getting ahead of yourself, she chided, then glanced toward Ned Nelson's cottage. Still dark. Where was Ned? She'd hoped to see him at the town meeting, she thought on a rush of guilt. It wasn't his fault, of course, but she'd had high hopes, given the spark of connection and friendship between them, that there'd also be attraction.

The man before her wiped Ned Nelson from her mind. Breath lodged midway down her throat as the dark stranger's hands slid under his waistband. She couldn't tear away her gaze as he slid the jeans over a smooth, tight backside, taking his briefs with them. Her heart was beating wildly out of control, and while she kept telling herself to leave, she knew there'd be plenty of time later to berate herself for spying. For now...

She bit down hard on her lower lip, masking a needy sound as he turned to face her. His skin was coppery in the moonlight, his nude body taut, the muscles rippling like water—sleek and animal. A thick, impossibly dark pelt raced downward, bisecting his pectorals, exploding into lusciously riotous curls that nestled the most intimate part of him. He wasn't aroused. But he wasn't soft, either. He was just hard enough that Pansy could guess how powerful he'd look if completely engorged.

Awed, she shuddered, dropped her sandals and simply stared as he turned away and slowly walked into the breakers. The back of him was every bit as nice as the front. He waited until the water lapped his upper thighs, then he dove, vanishing as gracefully as a fish beneath the water, moonlight catching on his back the way it might on scales. She'd never know how long she watched him at play—diving into the swells, then body surfing and riding the waves to shore while starlight danced on his skin.

It could have been minutes or hours, but finally he returned to shore, leaned and lifted his clothes from the sand. Only then did she realize her hands had splayed on her lower belly, as if something so simple could stop the ache he'd engendered there. Her hand inched lower. Her breath was trapped in her chest, and her heart was knocking hard. She'd never seen a man so perfect, never felt such an undeniable hunger to be touched...caressed ...held in an embrace. *He has to be a ghost*, she thought illogically. *This has to be destiny.*

Where was he going? she wondered, feeling strangely panicky. What if she never saw him again? He started walking down the beach, carrying his clothes, and once more, coming to her senses, Pansy glanced around. Ned Nelson's cottage was the only one near enough to walk to naked. And this man, she thought with a warm shiver, was very definitely not sweet, poetic Ned Nelson. No, Ned was the kind of man whose shoulder you cried on when a man like this left you. The kind who'd hand you a handkerchief embroidered with his initials.

The man's chin suddenly lifted. He turned sharply toward the dunes, and his eyes narrowed, piercing the darkness. He was staring right at the spot where she was hidden! And he had the look of an animal who'd just caught the scent of another on the wind. He leaned and, without taking his eyes from the dunes, shook sand from his jeans, stepped into them and fastened the fly.

Run! Pansy gasped. *He can't catch me!* What had she done? Had she really spied on him? Watched him swimming naked? Turning, she bolted without thinking, forgetting her sandals. Her heart was pounding, her face flushed with heat as she retraced her steps. Now that she was running, the soft sand impeded her movement. Her toes dived too deeply. Her heels sank. Every step plowed, spraying sand, and her calves started to burn, but she kept moving. Relief flooded her when she finally saw a far-off sand bluff she recognized. Another minute, and she'd be on Sand Road!

She was almost there when his low, sexy voice stopped her in her tracks. "Didn't you forget something?"

For a second, she considered not turning around, but the voice, like his looks, was so damn compelling. It was deep, calm and strangely familiar, as if she'd heard him speak a thousand times before this moment, maybe even felt his breath as he whispered in her ear. Yes, everything about him seemed foreign and yet so familiar....

She almost said, "Have we met?" But she didn't.

Maybe if she shut her eyes, then opened them again, he would vanish like a ghost. Maybe what happened here tonight was like the dune's surreal moonscape— more the domain of fantasy than reality. Deciding she'd better get out of there, she whirled to run, only to realize her lungs were already aching and burning. She didn't have the breath to take another step. She was suddenly aware of the scarlet heat in her cheeks. Well...he'd already caught her, right? She might as well face the music. Best to take the defensive, she thought, turning and arching a brow. "Excuse me? Did you say something?"

He was ten feet away, but the night was dark and the moon full, so the long shadow he cast nearly touched her bare feet. Almost impulsively, she reached down to catch the hem of her jewel-toned skirt. Caught by the sea breeze, it was flapping against her ankles and whipping dangerously upward, exposing her thighs. She grasped it, pressing her legs together to catch the fabric.

He was still wet, his black hair slicked away from his forehead. Saltwater drops glistened in his chest hair, like diamonds strewn in moss, and the sleeves of his shirt were loosely tied around his waist. He was wearing his sandals, carrying hers. Sand caked his feet. They were long, slender feet, strong-looking and well-formed. The kind of feet that might make a woman dream of kissing toes. And more, much more. She pushed away the image of him naked.

He was holding up her shoes. "These yours?"

Even from here, she could see that his eyes were the most compelling hazel. Not green, gray or blue, but a color that could become any of those. She registered their richness and depth, yes, but it was their kindness that pulled at her heart. "I must have left them in the sand," she managed, relieved there wasn't any indication in his gaze that he was speaking to a woman who'd been spying on him. He hardly sounded like a ghost, either. She quickly continued, "I...followed you earlier. I, uh, lost track of you for awhile there..." She paused, then emphasized, "Quite a long while, actually."

He didn't look convinced. In fact, his lip curled in a slight bemused smile that made his eyes dance. "Oh, really?"

"Oh, yes." She rushed on, unable to push away the vision of his body's lithe, graceful movements. "Uh...earlier, I saw you take the lottery board's letter from Zaw's. I was, uh, going to ask you about it. That's why I was following you."

He watched her curiously. "You were following me?"

"Well, yes," she said. As if that was the most reasonable thing in the world. It was better, she told herself, to play it that way.

As he stepped forward, probably to give her the sandals, her eyes were riveted to the dark arrowing chest hair that led to fascinating places she'd seen only moments before. She'd never been so aware of a man. She'd dated often and thought of herself as sexually healthy, but right now, her body felt truly electrified. Her knees weakened. Oh, God. Another wave of heat flooded her cheeks. Had she really just peeped on a stranger in the dunes? Even worse, was she standing here trying to have a normal conversation with him?

"Who are you?" She was glad her voice didn't quaver.

He'd come closer. He was five feet away, and he stopped and considered. With his head cocked and chin tilted downward, his truly marvelous face was accentuated. It was oval, sculpted, intense. His jaw was liberally coated with jet stubble that Pansy could easily imagine roughening her skin.

He studied her with those penetrating hazel eyes. "I am...who I am."

"Cryptic," she ventured, glad to hear her own wry tone, since it lent a sense of reality to this decidedly strange encounter.

"So, you followed me?" he prodded gently, his all-knowing expression more than unsettling.

"Yes," Pansy returned, belatedly realizing she sounded insistent, defensive. "But as I said, I lost track of you." *Yeah, right.*

"Well, you've found me."

"I've never seen you around here." She forced herself to continue, feeling nervous and half wishing he'd just hand over her sandals so she could leave. "And I know everyone on the island. I'm a Realtor, and I've rented to most people vacationing here. Who rented to you?"

"I'm...using a friend's place."

If so, the local Realtors would know that, too. She'd talked to Judith Hunt's team of cops, since she'd seen the boat explode, so Pansy knew this man wasn't affiliated with them. At least he wasn't a ghost, she thought, swallowing hard and feeling oddly giddy. Ever since she left the town meeting, she'd been wondering if she was losing her sanity. Suddenly, her heart missed a beat. Was this man connected with the explosion? But no, she decided. She'd never sensed a gentler, kinder presence, and Pansy had always trusted her instincts. "Which friend?" she forced herself to ask.

He smiled in flirtation. "You sure are nosy."

Maybe. But his withholding of information was exasperating. She chose to smile just as flirtatiously. "I saw you take the letter from Zaw's. Did you win the lottery?"

"Why do you want to know?"

"Just curious."

He offered a dazzling flash of white teeth. "Or maybe you have ways to spend my money, Pansy Hanley?"

He knew her name! How was that possible? "Do you know me?"

"You're a well-known Realtor," he said reasonably. "You just said so yourself."

She tried not to look offended. "Why would I want your money?"

"To buy Castle O'Lannaise?"

Watching this sexy stranger's nude swim had left her weak enough. That he knew her name was bothersome. But how could he know about her lifelong obsession with Castle O'Lannaise? How could a stranger be privy to things known only to those closest to her? It was as if he could see right through her!

It was definitely the wrong time for a cloud to pass over the moon, plunging them briefly into darkness. Another cloud came swiftly in its wake. Lacelike atmospheric moisture drew across the moon like a curtain as the stranger moved toward her again, and when he spoke, his voice was slow and lazy. Unmistakably seductive, it curled into her blood, roping into her limbs, as if to lasso her desire. "Be honest," he murmured. "Are you sure you've no plans for my money, *chèrie?*"

Chèrie? The world seemed to slide off-kilter. The night air seemed like a mirage. *Chèrie?* Wasn't that a French endearment? Her heart pounded. How did he know what she was thinking? If he really was the ghost of Jacques O'Lannaise, it was he—not her mind—who would become transparent! She could barely find her voice. "Of course I don't."

"Not even to buy Castle O'Lannaise?"

How could he know she'd hoped he'd buy it? Her heart was clamoring wildly. He stepped closer, then closer still. He was so close now that his eyes appeared less hazel, and more a dark smoky gray, like charcoal.

She swallowed hard. This was exactly how she'd always imagined Jacques O'Lannaise would look at her, his gaze drifting down the length of her—so leisurely, so aware—making her burn. As he dropped her sandals into the sand, she was smelling salt, and beneath that, something very, very male. Nothing floral, nothing soft, but a strong, almost animal scent that tunneled deep into her lungs, filling them and—for the briefest moment—making her want to beg him to love her. Right here, right now, she wanted to say.

But that was crazy! She shouldn't be having these feelings for a stranger! No man, certainly not one she'd met on a beach, should pull this kind of wild, inexplicable passion from her! Her voice, no longer strong, came out with a shiver. "Who are you?"

He was taller than she, and he gazed down, his eyes

touched by real tenderness. His words were almost a whisper. "I think you know."

He was a stranger, and yet the deeper she looked into his hazel eyes, the more she was sure she had met him before, if only in her dreams. "I know you, don't I?" she managed to ask uncertainly, feeling overwhelmed and dizzy.

Again, that low seductive voice found her ears. "Do you want to know me?"

"Who are you?" she whispered again.

His eyes were hot on her skin, burning as they dragged downward, starting with a greedy perusal of her face, then drifting to the slender length of her neck, then her breasts, the tips of which tightened. She told herself she was glad when that gaze moved upward once more, settling on her mouth, and yet... Well, she'd never had a man look at her quite this hungrily and, if the truth be told, she didn't much mind.

"What if I told you I was Jacques O'Lannaise?" he murmured, raising a finger and stroking it down her cheek.

Her lips parted to tell him to quit teasing her, but his finger stopped on her mouth, and she said nothing, just kept her lips parted as if for a kiss. She thought of her ancestor, Iris, standing on the deck of the *Destiny*, her lips parted in just this way the second before Jacques's mouth claimed hers.

"Did you enjoy watching me swim, *chèrie*?"

So, he knew! The remaining breath left her lungs. Before she found her voice to answer, his eyes lit with amusement and he chuckled softly, and then he simply traced the finger over her lips, learning the contours. A soft sigh escaped between them when he dropped his hand. Another when he turned away and began walking into the dunes.

"Wait," she murmured.

He didn't stop. Mindlessly, she bolted after him, and when she reached him, she grasped his arm, the quiver of bare skin under her fingertips feeling like an electrical current. As he stopped in his tracks, then turned to face her, she softly whispered, "Wait!"

His eyes found hers. "For what, *chèrie?*"

"I don't know," she said, breathing hard. "But I—" The deepening warmth in his eyes gave her no more comfort than the parting of his lips or the huskiness of his voice. How could she explain? Even though he was a stranger, she didn't want him to go.

His gaze assessed her. "I think it's you who's waiting."

He seemed to know what he was talking about. Funny, she thought. It was her voice that sounded ethereal and ghostly, as flighty as the wind. "Me waiting? For what?"

Large strong hands, warm from the sea, circled her back, and her silk blouse was drenched as he hauled her against a hard bare chest, wet from salt water. "For a kiss like fire," he whispered.

Breath feathered her cheek then, his excited pant matching hers as he tilted his chin and angled his head down. A second passed—warm, firm lips hovered— and then the stranger closed his mouth masterfully over hers.

4

REX'S MIND hazed with need as his lips fastened more firmly to Pansy's. Had playing the role of Jacques O'Lannaise put something magical into the kiss? Something transcending reason? Was Pansy's ghost real—and somehow holding Rex under his spell, compelling him to act?

No, he thought. That was whimsy talking, the voice of Rex's poetic soul. As shudders rippled down his wet back, he uttered a soft moan. The kiss was spontaneous. Combustive. It erupted like a volcano, then flowed like lava. Pansy was already kissing him back with everything she had, and their lips swelled together like ocean waves. Her tongue dived, his delved, until the kiss itself was a wave—rising, falling, undulating. Emotions moved within the kiss, elusive and graceful.

At the first touch of their mouths, it was clear they'd be good together. And now, feeling deliciously dark, hot liquid seemed to rush through Rex, racing through his veins. Had this woman really been enjoying watching his naked swim?

The notion aroused him beyond belief. She was so adventuresome. Exactly the kind of woman he'd always dreamed of. Tightening his arms around her back, he forced their hips closer.

One more inch, he thought, and she'd feel him

swelling with passion. He went for it, and as their hips locked, she shook and gasped. He was shaking, too. And when he flexed his fingers on the watery silk of her blouse, grasping a fistful and using it to urge her even nearer, his soul cried out.

"Impossible," he whispered, his tone incredulous, his voice ragged.

"What?"

She was impossible. Too good to be true. But because he couldn't find the right words, he didn't answer, only deepened the kiss. How could he explain this gripping compulsion to touch all her softer places? Or the drive to be inside a woman he barely knew?

Right now, he felt he'd die, burn up without her. He feather kissed her mouth, then brought more pressure, and as the renewed ministrations further parted her lips, he heard the ocean roar in his ears. Suddenly, he was drowning in taste and heat and images of sensual surrender. He'd never felt anything like this. Which meant maybe she was right. Maybe they were touched by destiny. Maybe when Rex decided to play the pirate, he'd tempted fate.

Ever since, he hadn't felt like himself. Infused by haunted passion, he raked his mouth across hers. Already, he was tasting the lush slopes of her breasts and feeling their buds constrict between his lips. He couldn't wait to trace the curves of her hips with his tongue and lick the backs of her knees. After that, he'd tease apart her thighs and kiss everything between.

Their bellies brushed, hips cradled, and slow, dark heat flared once more. Her mouth slackened on his, and as desire melted through her bones like candle wax, she went languid in his arms. For a breathless second, he became aware of the romance of the night surrounding them—the yellow moon, dazzling stars, crashing waves and hot sand that oozed like butter between the toes of their bare feet.

He tried to pull himself back to reality. But this wasn't reality. At least these weren't average, first-kiss circumstances. He tried to tell himself that Pansy only wanted him because she was lost in the fantasy that he was Jacques O'Lannaise, her dream lover and pirate ghost.

But he didn't care.

Maybe she wanted some damn phantom, not him, the real him, but right now, he couldn't dwell on it. He'd been in lust with this woman since their first conversation, and now that his hungry mouth was on hers, he meant to offer whatever he could to entice his goddess to stay.

Rex always met women on his vacations, and he always dreamed something would last. Nothing ever had. And while it was true he wanted a soul mate, maybe it was time to try a fling instead of risking disappointment when there was no end-of-the-rainbow future. "Are you going to keep letting me kiss you, *chèrie?*" he murmured against her mouth. What he meant was, *Can we take this further?*

"Yes," she whispered.

Despite the unusual circumstances in which he was pretending to be Jacques O'Lannaise, she sounded so, well, down to earth. Warm and willing. Ready and able. He'd never dreamed something like this could happen. Wasn't she going to ask who he was? Didn't she care that he was a stranger? A man she'd met on a beach? Or did she have such powers of imagination that she really believed he was Jacques?

His heart was hammering, pounding high up in his throat as she let him sweep his tongue upward on her neck. Ridges of his teeth teased, then he butterflied a silken hollow behind her ear, eliciting a soft sigh from her. He felt a blow to his lower gut when his tongue headed south, dipping inside her blouse. Mint that tasted like after-dinner tea hit his consciousness like a sledgehammer. Dammit, skin wasn't supposed to taste like mint! Lower, he tasted salt. Lower still, he found the beginning crest of her breasts, soft swells that looked like the sweet, white rim of a margarita glass.

Mindlessly, he whispered, "*Chèrie*," sighing against the building pressure of jeans that had gotten bothersomely tight. He shifted away, unable to take any more contact as he splayed a hand on her chest. Fanning his fingers, he saw they fully spanned her collarbone.

Their eyes met. Hers were steady, imploring. In what he took as a gesture of surrender, she tipped back her head, so he could glide his fingers upward, cradle her slender neck, then stroke soft skin. Pads of fingers explored, and he was glad she didn't protest as his tongue continued its gentle, downward caress. "I want to drag you down to the ocean, *chèrie*," he murmured, his tongue languorously traveling down... down...until his teeth circled the top button of her blouse. He popped it open with his mouth.

"The ocean?" she echoed huskily in the seductive voice that had ghosted in his mind since their first conversation.

"Make love to you in the water," he assured, his voice turning gravelly. "In the waves."

When he'd seen her standing barefoot in the sand with the night breeze pressing her silk blouse and skirt to her skin, his mouth had gone bone dry. She was so damn lovely, he'd thought. So pretty it almost hurt, somehow. His heart had swelled as he took in how her clothes had outlined every tempting curve. That's when he'd decided to pretend he was Jacques. Oh, he'd considered it before, when they met at Casa Eldora, but now he knew he had to see Pansy live her fantasy.

She'd started the game, after all. Even now, he could remember the feel of her eyes on his back as he swam—hot, steady and intent. He'd shrugged off the sensation. He was a cop. What he'd seen on the mean streets had made him too suspicious, he told himself. Besides, he possessed overly sensitive radar since he was born and bred in Manhattan. And he was here due to his father's disappearance, something that had left him edgy.

But she'd been watching him.

A satisfied rumble sounded in his chest as he unbuttoned another button, again with his teeth. It was almost like a sickness, he decided—this insistent, gnawing urge to possess her mouth and taste her skin. The artery at her neck was wild beneath his fingers, pulsing, and soon the tails to her shirt caught the wind and flapped outward like the wings of a bird. Vaguely, he was aware that his chest, still wet from the sea, had drenched the blouse he'd been intent on removing. He gazed at where puckered silk had opened, exposing the bra she wore beneath. Against white lace, he watched her nipples reacting—

She shivered. "I'm cold."

"Aroused," he corrected, his hot eyes gazing at the effect of chill salt water and the heat of kisses. In a flash fantasy, he suddenly saw himself dragging her into the crashing surf while peeling off her sea-soaked clothes. Swallowing hard against the sudden cottony dryness of his mouth, he drew in a raspy breath as he unhooked the front clasp of the bra. For a second, he could swear his heart stopped beating. Then he murmured, "You're beautiful, *chèrie*," as he pushed the bra cups back toward her shoulders.

The peaking buds were stiff and straining in the night wind, damp from his drenched chest and ready for more wet heat from his mouth. As he delivered it—offering hot, honeyed kisses that swirled dizzily around the nipples—a heady scent filled his lungs, of close moist air and wildflowers that thrived in the dunes...rising pungent scents of her musk that Rex knew would haunt him forever.

Her knees gave out then. Just like that. With no warning. He caught her, the swiftly tightening arm that braced her back mindlessly lifting her. Their hips slammed, joining in a way that rocked his world. She was swollen where he ached for her. Heat shivered through him when he realized how much she was throbbing for him. Her thighs, as promising as an invitation, quivered, and his went taut as he braced, gritting his teeth in both agony and pleasure as he continued registering her soft female heat.

Rex knew he wasn't a ghost. He was flesh and blood, but it was hard to believe Pansy Hanley hadn't been fashioned from something magical. Long lengths of bone comprised her enticing frame. Cushioning feminine curves yielded to the steady pressure of his harder body as a man might expect—and yet something about her remained maddeningly elusive. Like the salt-touched air or nearby water stretching around them for countless miles, she seemed to flow around him.

He saw a very definite future. Pleasure flashed in his mind—her lying naked in the surf, the sea foam rushing over her belly and frothing between her legs as he licked away salty drops…and then her lowering herself over him, her knees digging soft pockets in the sand beside his thighs as she straddled him, taking him firmly in her hands, her mouth…

The woman was pure rapture. Poetry, he thought as he suckled her breasts, knowing he was driving her toward the edge with the ravenously fierce pull of his mouth. Everything around them had gone strangely silent. The wind had ceased. Gulls quit crying. He couldn't hear waves breaking on shore. Nothing seemed to exist except for the place where his firm mouth had locked—small, hot, liquid.

"Heavenly," he groaned.

His groin was pulsing. Engorged and hard, his erection was surging against his fly. He wanted Pansy so bad it was painful. He was kissing both breasts now, his tongue flickering between them, his palms lifting them high, his whispered sweet nothings serving as the warm assurance that he'd soon demand more.

Now, he thought, knowing neither of them could take much more. His hands tightened—one tenderly squeezing a breast, another lowering from her neck to caress an arm—thin, long, bare, he noted—a shudder racking his shoulders when the silk of her skirt rustled with a whisper of suggestion. Undress me.

He wasn't about to argue. Fingers bracketing her spine, he leaned back a fraction, studying the inward nip of an impossibly tiny waist. Tenderly, he cupped his palms as they slid downward, molding her hips. If she was going to stop him, she'd better do it soon. Lord, was she really going to let a supposed stranger make love to her?

He caressed her backside. With watery silk rippling under his sensitized fingers, he could feel her vibrating. Restrained tension was locked inside her. In his mouth, her tongue was wild and uncontrollable when he kissed her again. She was meeting him thrust for thrust, the kiss breaking over them like sun-hot surf as he urged her to lie on the ground, the soft slope of a dune absorbing the impact of their bodies. He lay half beside her, half on top, his knee gently nestling in silk, parting her legs.

From the way she stared at him, he guessed her flood of desire was about to burst. Her lips were red, swollen and wet. His heart aching, he took her in—the high, firm, uncovered breasts, the stark wariness in her eyes that said she wasn't a hundred percent sure he was even real.

"Who are you?" she croaked.

The night breeze meshed with his voice. "Does it matter?"

Her breath hitched. "I don't know. Maybe. How do you know things about me?"

"I just do." Leaning, he nuzzled her neck. "I know what you'll like," he murmured. "What you won't..."

Her hips arched from the cushioning sand, seeking him. "How?"

"Don't worry." The words turned ragged, and he gasped as he pressed against her side, knowing she could feel him, burning and hard. "I'm...safe," he assured. That's what she wanted to hear, and it was true. He even had a condom with him, tucked in his back pocket with his badge. He always carried condoms, if only to hand out to prostitutes he met in the street while working. "I'm going to be something else, too, Pansy."

Her chest was exposed to the night air, and in their tussle, the button of her skirt had come undone. Hungry eyes locked on his lips. "What are you going to be?"

"Your dream lover," he whispered. "Your seducer."

Trailing his fingers, he dragged down the skirt's zipper, knowing he'd never seen a woman who looked more in need of living out a fantasy. Clutching a handful of sun-spun gold, he used the strands of her hair to urge her head back just as the wraparound skirt opened. Jewel-patterned fabric caught in the wind, opening like a sail and forming a blanket beneath her. She was wearing simple white lace bikinis with pink rosebuds adorning the sides.

With a quick inhalation, he shifted his weight and moved between her legs. Salty droplets from his hair fell like rain, sprinkling her cheeks, spattering between her lips as he dragged his mouth across hers. But as he tongued away salty drops, more fell, and the pointed tip of his tongue raced after one in particular, licking right behind it. By the time he was done, he'd licked so far down that his tongue was in her navel.

She whimpered, the sound needy and feminine as his hand molded the panties. She was so full where he cupped her that his fingers couldn't close over all the wet lace. He glided a palm under the waistband, then gasped when he discovered she was slick.

She reached for him, too. He felt her sharp inward breath on his lips as she caressed him through his jeans, and when his mouth closed on hers, it was in a claiming kiss of almost savage male triumph. Trailing a languid, sizzling thread of heat downward, he stripped off her panties. Despite that, he knew he was loving her too slowly—they were both panting hard, overwhelmed with need—but the truth was, Rex never wanted this to end.

Another cry—this one throatier, deeper—was torn from her damp, parted lips as he pushed a finger inside her, and hearing her cry, he felt his heart hammer. Sucking a breath through his teeth, he moved the caressing hand that was fondling him through his jeans, making him feel sure he'd explode. He shucked the pants, then found the condom, careful she wouldn't see his badge.

He edged on top of her. Heat found heat. He throbbed at the portal, and then with the power of his first thrust, he went deep, driving into her womb, pressing her into the waiting, cushioning sand. With another thrust she was pushed further into dark, alluring shadows that the moon cast on the walls of sand surrounding them.

The night was beautiful, the stars gleaming as they pierced a velvet sky. He felt her thread her hands deep into his hair, grasping the strands in fistfuls as he guided her hips. She twisted in a joining that threatened his control. A current of fire seemed to race through his blood, his head swam, and his senses drowned.

She was his. Tonight. Near a public beach in the sand. As he rolled his hips, he stroked her lips with his tongue and teased the ridges of her teeth and the silken pockets of her cheek. As his mind blanked, he thought of how she'd spied on him, stealthily following him into these surreal dunes on a dark night.

Oh, he didn't like that she'd wanted to use him as a buyer for her precious castle. Just once, he wanted to be sought for the man he really was...the man he usually kept hidden from the world. The man who, deep down, was probably a lot like good old Ned Nelson.

But right now, it didn't matter.

She was shuddering. They were both about to come, and blood whistled through his veins like wind in the dunes as her legs wrapped around his waist. "You want him, don't you?" he whispered shakily, sucking pleasure from her neck like sweet candy.

"Who?" she gasped.

"Me...Jacques O'Lannaise."

"You're not Jacques O'Lannaise...you can't be."

His hoarse words came in a soft, sexy patter. "I'm your pirate, Pansy. Your lover in the dunes. Your magic..."

Moments from now, he'd start to wonder what he'd done. He'd leave her in the sand to gather her clothes, wondering whether she'd really been ravished by a ghost lover. But now he reached between them with a flattened palm and glided a thumb to her bud. At the same time, his weight pushed him deeper, opening her with strokes of pleasure that made her writhe.

"*Chèrie*," he urged, his free hand dragging into the cascading river of her hair. Rushing sounded in his ears—his own blood or the ocean, he wasn't sure—as she suddenly gushed, breaking on his shore with a startled cry of ecstasy.

He captured the intimate moment with a kiss, the push of his tongue melding with her unbroken cry. The push of his hips sent him toward joining her in oblivion. Over and over, he threaded his fingers into her hair, then deeper, into the warm sand as he broke, frothing inside her. And as he came, his own cry said tonight was just the beginning.

5

"LOOKS LIKE Lou Fairchild and your sister Lily are hitting it off," said Ned Nelson conversationally as he guided Pansy in a waltz across the concrete floor of the candlelit pavilion. "Not to mention Vi and that guy Garth Garrison."

"Yes," she murmured absently, unable to draw her gaze away from where it was fixed over Ned's shoulder on Castle O'Lannaise in the distance. Her breath suddenly caught. Had a shadow just passed in one of the estate's darkened windows? Was someone inside? Or was it only a cloud passing above the sandy bluff? Maybe a flash of light from the lighthouse?

Her heart was hammering, beating out of control, and she took a deep, calming breath, hoping to still it. Just shadows, she told herself. A shiver that had little to do with the warm, sultry night breeze wended slowly down her spine, feeling like a drop of hot water...or a man's tongue. She pushed away the thought.

"I can't believe Garth Garrison lives on the island," Ned continued. "I've never read any of his books, but I know people who have. Especially *Bloodsuckers*."

"Right," Pansy managed to say, her throat feeling tight, her body flooding with sensations and memories left by a nameless man she didn't know, a stranger she'd met only briefly on a dark, deserted beach.

Was he even real? Pansy wasn't sure. After they'd

made love, she'd awakened, still unclothed and lying on her skirt, which she instinctively wrapped around herself. Even now, she could swear he'd remained there, watching from the shadows. Maybe it was her imagination, but he'd seemed to hover like a protective, dark avenging angel who'd swoop down and rescue her if anyone happened upon her, sleeping in the dunes.

"Are you there?" she had called, her voice catching.

Only the roar of the breaking surf answered. And then the fleeting sixth sense of the man's presence had vanished. It was pointless to chase him—she'd known she'd never find him unless he wanted to be found—so she'd gone home. When she couldn't reach Ned by phone to cancel their appointment, she'd changed clothes and gone to the bonfire to meet him.

That was a week ago. Now, nightly, the stranger had haunted her dreams, filling her world with wildly erotic images. Would she ever see him again? Who was he? She was burning with the need to know.

"Wasn't it on the *New York Times* list?" Ned prompted.

"Hmm?" Pansy tried, but still couldn't pull her eyes away from Castle O'Lannaise. Perched on its craggy bluff, it looked forlorn and mysterious tonight, and like the man who'd built it so many years ago, it was undeniably compelling.

Pansy felt an illogical, almost visceral pull to wander there, under the wide, vaulting arches of the equestrian breeding lodge and the galleries of horse stalls beyond, past columns of adobe that shone under the moon. She drew another deep breath. No, whatever shadows she'd seen were only that—shadows, the kind a woman always saw on a fire-lit, velvet night.

The man she'd met was real, as substantial as wood, concrete or stone, and the idea that a pirate ghost had materialized was utterly ridiculous. Her two sisters would tell her to have her head examined! Not that she—practical, levelheaded Pansy—would ever tell them what she'd done.

"What?" she suddenly asked.

"*Bloodsuckers*. Wasn't it a bestseller?"

"I think so."

"I'd like to meet Garth. I headed his way earlier, but then Vi snagged him for a dance."

"I'll introduce you. And let me talk to Vi. Maybe we'll have a cookout and invite you guys. That way, you can mingle. Not that my cooking could ever compare to yours." She chuckled. "Almond butter on rye is one of my better specialties."

"Invite me over, and I'll bring homemade jam."

"Homemade?"

He nodded. "My jumble-berry jam's out of this world."

She believed him. "Where'd you learn to cook?"

"Watching my mother."

She smiled at him. Endearing, she thought, noting the caring tone. "You have a good relationship?"

"The best," he said without a second's hesitation. The sense of family closeness warmed her, and without realizing it, she shifted physically closer to Ned as they danced.

"Siblings?" she asked.

"Two brothers."

"And I've got two sisters," she returned, liking that sense of connection. "Are you close with them, too?"

"Like crossed fingers," he said grinning, and for the next two dances he proved it, amusing her with stories about growing up. She told him about her past, too, and when she mentioned the loss of her parents in a boating accident when she was young, Ned didn't say all the wrong things, as so many people did. Instead, he asked her how she felt about what had happened.

She shrugged. "You get used to it here. They got caught in a summer squall. Really," she added, "when you think about it, the Hanleys haven't lost that many people. Just Iris's family and my parents. Given that we've been on the island nearly three hundred years, I guess it's to be expected." She shot him a wry smile. "I do wish it hadn't been them. I cherish the memories I have."

When they fell silent again, she was surprised to find that she'd snuggled almost into his embrace. They were dancing chest to chest, and his thighs were ghosting against hers, softly brushing. She told herself to move away, since it wasn't fair to lead him on if she wasn't interested in a physical relationship. Oh, she thought, she might have warmed to Ned if it hadn't been for the stranger on the beach....

After a moment, she realized Ned was squinting at her.

"Are you okay?" he asked.

Hearing the concern in his tone infused her with guilt. Ned was so incredibly sweet. Misinterpreting her distraction, he kept assuming she was still upset over witnessing the explosion aboard the *Destiny*. "Yes," she said. "I'm fine."

"Why don't I believe you?"

Pulling herself firmly to the present, Pansy drew her eyes from Jacques O'Lannaise's estate, flashed Ned a quick smile and surveyed their surroundings. "Because you're a mother hen."

On the beach, a bonfire flared, and mingling vacationers huddled around picnic tables in the sand, eating chicken wings and chips while a six-piece local band, complete with a man who strummed a washboard, played a waltz. "Well," added Ned conversationally, "Ms. Hunt sure seems to know what she's doing."

Realizing her mind had drifted again, Pansy blinked. Why couldn't she concentrate on what Ned was saying? He was such a nice, sweet guy. Over the past week, since they'd first met, she'd spent so much time getting to know him. "I'm sorry," she apologized, her eyes settling where his shaggy blond hair dipped into eyes that were shielded by black-framed glasses, the nosepiece of which he'd broken yesterday and fixed with tape. As she looked at him, a lopsided grin suddenly tilted her lips.

He seemed pleased. "Whatcha smiling at?"

She shrugged. "Nothing." But just looking at Ned Nelson did strange things to her heart. Why, she didn't know. Maybe because he was the kind of guy who said "whatcha" and "you bet."

Besides, he was so obviously in need of a woman. His usually rumpled clothes were all wrong for him— oversize khaki pants and wild Hawaiian shirts in colors no one wore anymore. This evening's offering was a disastrous collage of bursting sunflowers in burnt orange, hot pink and chocolate brown. Every time she looked at him, Pansy felt the urge to take him shopping.

Surveying him and shaking her head, she wondered how a man living in Manhattan had managed not to learn any sense of personal style. Strange, she thought, as she continued moving against him in the waltz, the way he danced almost made her suspect there was a he-man body under all those bad clothes, too.

"Sorry," she suddenly repeated, coming to her senses a final time and registering the strong warmth of his hand as he settled it on her waist. "I really can't concentrate tonight, can I? Did you say something, Ned?"

"Just that I've had fun with you this week, Pansy."

Wishing away the thoughts her mystery man had left ghosting in her mind, she shot Ned another answering smile. "Me, too. It's been fun."

She'd run into Ned at every turn—in Zaw's and on the beach—and they'd talked about art and poetry, something she usually found men incapable of, especially on an island populated by crusty fishermen. One day, she'd stopped where Ned had set up his easel in the sand. When she'd tried to urge him downwind, where Judith Hunt's investigation wasn't marring the landscape, he'd merely grinned. "That's the great thing about painting," he'd assured her, "it has nothing to do with reality. I can brush out whatever I wish."

"But you won't," she'd teased.

He'd glanced toward the boat's wreckage, chuckled and said, "Probably not."

The fact was, Ned Nelson had turned out to be a cop groupie. Every time he took a break from painting, he'd carry a pitcher of his homemade lemonade—it was far less tart than Pansy's—down to the crime scene, and then he'd chew the fat with Judith Hunt for awhile. On that particular day, Pansy had felt charmed and hungry enough to accept his dinner invitation, and although she wasn't conscious of feeling any sparks of attraction, she'd stayed long after they'd finished the fish fillets he'd masterfully cooked in dry white wine.

Chalk another one up for Ned Nelson, Pansy thought. He might not be a looker, but he could cook like Emeril. She sighed. The truth was, when she'd stayed that night, talking into the wee hours, she'd also been hoping for some distraction, since searching for her mystery man had been fruitless.

Some tourists were rumored to have spotted the island's famous ghost, but Pansy had tried not to get too excited, since that happened every summer. After doing some checking, she'd realized no Realtor had rented to a man meeting the description, and no one knew of a dark-haired man who was using the cottage of a friend.

Which left Castle O'Lannaise. Was the man up there? Glancing furtively in that direction, she took in the red tile roofs that glinted in the moonlight.

"You're okay?" Ned murmured again, following her gaze.

"Absolutely."

The waltz ended, and he placed a hand gingerly on

her back, guiding her toward the buffet tables. "Are you sure? You seem...so distracted tonight."

She tore her gaze from the castle once more. "People have been saying they've seen...Jacques O'Lannaise walking on the beach," she offered.

"So I hear."

Pansy's sister Lily claimed she'd overheard a group of three female tourists in her stationery store say they'd seen a rakish man on the beach by the lighthouse pier. At first, Pansy had assumed Lily was teasing her, until she'd overheard three women in Zaw's discussing the ghost sighting. According to them, they had corroboration, since six-year-old Harlin Gills, who was vacationing with his parents, had also sworn he'd seen Jacques—and at last week's town meeting, no less!

The poor, deluded grade schooler had vowed that the ghost had winked at him, Pansy reminded herself, shaking her head in disbelief. "The rumors aren't true, of course," she said.

"Oh, I wouldn't be so sure," teased Ned.

"Well, those women and little Harlin Gills saw someone," Pansy conceded. "Do you think Ms. Hunt believes this, uh, supposed ghost could be a suspect?" Pansy couldn't help but ask, feeling compelled to voice her darkest fears. Not that Pansy believed the man had anything to do with *Destiny*'s explosion, not given the cherished way he'd loved her body.

Ned shook his head as they reached a picnic table, then he handed Pansy a plate and nodded toward Judith Hunt, who was down by the bonfire. "Nope. Ms. Hunt says it's just tourists reacting to all the local lore," he assured.

Pansy followed his gaze, squinting thoughtfully. The female officer was stunningly beautiful, tall and regal. Long black hair hung past her shoulders, and she possessed penetrating dark blue eyes that usually stared, unblinking, from a pale, oval face. Her lips were unusually well-defined, and she always kept them perfectly lipsticked in shocking crimson. At their first meeting, Pansy had been startled, since the woman would have looked at home on a New York runway, but when she'd questioned Pansy, that impression changed. Between the piercing eyes and throaty, alto voice that was cool even for a professional's, Pansy understood the woman was one-hundred-percent cop.

"Are you sure you're not still thinking about that explosion?"

Pansy's heart lurched, doing a surprising flip-flop as Ned put an extra chicken wing on her plate. "No. And please stop worrying about me," she added. "I'm flattered, but..."

"It's possible you're not over the shock."

"But I am," she defended. She should have known Ned would misread her absentmindedness, but she could hardly tell him about her interlude with the stranger on the beach. "I mean, seeing the explosion was traumatic," she clarified.

"I'll bet."

Countless times this week, Ned had talked with her about the details of what she'd experienced that night—the sudden, deafening boom that had awakened her, the instinctive rush to the French doors of her room, which opened onto a patio, the wrenching feeling of powerlessness as she'd watched the *Destiny* upend and sink, knowing someone aboard might be in need of help. "Actually," she ventured, telling as much as she could, "it's the ghost sightings. You know how I feel about our local legends. What if someone really has seen Jacques?"

That brought a bemused smile to his lips. "Ah. I should have known."

She swallowed hard, wanting his help but not wanting to expose herself. "Would you go up there with me? To the estate?"

He squinted. "I know I said I wanted to explore the place, but you're the Realtor. Why do you need me?"

She wasn't quite sure. She wanted to see her dream lover again. She feared she never would. However, if she did, she wanted to know something about him, preferably starting with his name. "Protection?" she suggested, the idea that her ghost could have been involved in the explosion still niggling.

"I doubt you need it," Ned returned. "Given the dreamy look in your eyes whenever you mention your ghost, I'd only be a third wheel."

Something in his tone made her glance up too quickly and register the teasing, knowing glint in his eye. For the briefest second, she wondered if he'd seen her with the stranger. After all, they'd been near Ned's cottage. But no...that was just her guilty mind at work. "Don't be silly," Pansy retorted. "Besides, I meant just in case I ran into anybody involved in the boat's explosion."

His expression turned grim. "Ms. Hunt says they've recovered enough evidence to show it was sabotage, not a mechanical failure."

Despite the seriousness of the conversation, she bit

back a smile, since Ned, always deferential to both women and the police, had never referred to Judith Hunt by her first name. Then worry overtook her. "They still don't know who was on board, right?"

He shook his head. "If so, they haven't released names to the public."

"The water's shallow enough they'd have found...bodies."

"That's what Ms. Hunt said."

Pansy blew out a sigh. "I wish I could remember something helpful." She hated to think she'd missed a detail, however small, that could help solve a crime. "I wish I'd seen someone come ashore."

"Me, too," he said simply.

Something in his tone made her react. "You're really interested in this case, aren't you."

"No," he defended. "Not particularly."

He was lying, and once more, her heart squeezed for Ned Nelson. Not being the macho type, she guessed he felt drawn into the atmosphere of intrigue and danger surrounding the wreck site. Didn't he know some women liked beta, not alpha, men? If she was more the beta man type, she'd definitely go for him.

"Well, maybe some memories will come back to you eventually," Ned suggested softly.

Doubtful, she thought. Since the night of the explosion, she'd spent hours racking her brain. "Well, anyway," she continued, shrugging as if to dispel the topic, "you did say you wanted to explore my castle, right?"

"Yeah. I did." A sudden sparkle lit his eyes, almost

as if he was privy to a private joke. "But like I say, I don't know if I can compete with your ghost."

"Don't worry," she returned with a playful laugh. "You've got a few things to recommend you."

Looking surprised, Ned said, "Such as?"

"You're alive," Pansy quipped. "And the ghost isn't."

When he laughed, his teeth flashed. Straight and white, they were, in Pansy's opinion, Ned Nelson's best feature. "That's a start."

"We'll have to go in the early evening, since I've got work during the week and the tour bus on weekends. I'm not free for the next couple of nights, but I can go any day after that, around five. When can you make it?"

He named the day, and then his eyes turned serious as he glanced upward, taking in the estate that had been shrouded in so much mystery. A shadow seemed to pass in his eyes, and for a second, his expression bothered her. He was looking toward the buildings almost as if they could be an adversary, and yet the impression was so fleeting that she shrugged it off.

"If you stop by and pick me up," he said, "I'll make you dinner."

Any tension she felt dissipated as a chuckle erupted from her lips. She was starting to feel spoiled rotten by this man. "I can't impose again."

"A woman like you could never be an imposition," he assured. She told herself to refrain—after all, she didn't have any interest in Ned, did she? Nevertheless, she couldn't help but rise to the bait of flirtation. "A woman like me?"

His lips twitched with merriment, but instead of listing her positive attributes, which was what she expected, he said, "If it makes you feel better, you can set up that cookout with Garth Garrison." His smile deepened. "Maybe we could even invite Ms. Hunt."

She was amused. "You absolutely love listening to all that cop talk, don't you?"

He seemed to hesitate. "I find it fascinating."

She eyed him curiously. "Have you ever met cops before?"

He considered for what seemed an inordinate amount of time. "Nope. This is a first for me."

"Then we'll invite Ms. Hunt." Once more, she told herself not to flirt with Ned, but somehow she couldn't help herself. She sighed heavily. "Of course, I don't know how I can compete with her."

At that, Ned laughed. "As near as I can tell, you've got a few things to recommend you over Ms. Hunt."

"Such as?" she quipped, echoing his previous words.

He gave a throaty, pleasant chuckle. He, too, said, "You're alive."

"You're terrible," she chastised. Then she conceded, "She isn't the warmest woman, is she?"

"Hardly."

Something in his tone—or was it his voice?—brought Pansy's eyes to his again. For the briefest instant, his voice had sounded familiar, and she tilted her head. She felt as if she was trying to think of a word that was right on the tip of her tongue. He'd reminded her of someone...but who?

"What?" he said.

"Nothing." Shaking her head to dispel the odd sensation, Pansy finished her wings, tossed the paper plate into the trash along with his, then said, "We should probably go soon. Get a good night's sleep."

He was eyeing her curiously. "Are you sure you're not thinking about that explosion? You seem preoccupied, and when I asked, Ms. Hunt said that can be a sign of posttraumatic stress."

Putting her hands on her hips, Pansy stared at him pointedly. "I'm fine," she repeated a final time.

He didn't look convinced. "No nightmares?"

No. Her sleeping mind was filled with images that were tender, sensual and unforgettable. She shook her head. "Only dreams," she promised. That was the truth.

His eyes settled on hers. "I hope those dreams will be good tonight."

She smiled. Poor Ned Nelson had no idea what spicy erotica he was referring to. "Oh—" she couldn't help but think of her mystery man "—judging from the past few nights, I'm sure my dreams will all be doozies."

REX WAS even more sure than Pansy that her dreams would be memorable, since he planned to make them that way. Witnessing the boat's explosion was traumatic, of course, just as she'd said, and he wished for the sake of his family that she'd remember something, but he was also sure her distraction was due to reliving the sex they'd had on the beach the previous week.

Rex was having the same problem.

He tucked her into her black compact and shut the door. As she roared down the sandy, shell-lined road, he waved and began considering his next move. All week, he'd told himself to write off what happened between him and Pansy as a one-time event. Pretending to be her fantasy pirate was bad enough, but to keep up the pretense would be unconscionable. Especially since Rex liked her so much. They shared favorite authors, artists and foods, and while she obviously didn't feel sexually attracted to Ned Nelson, they'd sure hit it off.

Their minds were simpatico. And yet her body called to him. Should he tell her who he was? Risk Judith Hunt's throwing him off the island when it might jeopardize his chance to find his father?

No. His family was counting on him. Every time Rex thought of his mother's heartbreak, he became more determined to find Augustus—and soon. He'd have to stay quiet. But Pansy's touch and taste beckoned him. He couldn't go another night without her. She was like a searchlight from the lighthouse when the steamy tide turned landward and the hot nights melted into gray-fog dawns.

Night after night, he'd lain awake, staring past where the police worked, listening to waves lap the shore, remembering how she'd felt in his arms. Sometimes, he'd imagine her bedroom. She'd have a four-poster bed, he decided. Pastel walls. Carpet so thick he'd feel as if his feet were melting.

No doubt, he was wrong, but years of training had made him a good cop, which meant he wanted the truth about who she was and how she lived. Besides, given how many times Pansy's eyes had traveled to Castle O'Lannaise while they were dancing, their nighttime tryst was never far from her mind, either. Maybe it was time to create some new memories.

Shutting his eyes, Rex blew out a breath. Once more, his open palms were gliding along her thighs. Once more, he was leaning, his lips locking around the peaks of aroused breasts. "No doubt about it," he whispered. Tonight he had no choice. He was going to Pansy Hanley's bedroom. He'd brought his lock pick set, so it would be easy enough to break in.

Releasing a soft curse when the ringing cell phone interrupted his thoughts, he dug in the pocket of the baggy khakis and withdrew it. "Yeah," he said, glancing over his shoulder, hoping Judith Hunt wouldn't notice him taking the call. After all, Ned Nelson wasn't exactly a glued-to-his-cell-phone type.

"That's no way to answer a phone. Haven't you heard of hello?"

It was Truman. "Sorry. I'm preoccupied, little brother."

"Good. That means you're busy. What have you found out?"

"Not much." Rex caught Truman up on his most recent activities, the tone of the conversation tense because another week had passed since Augustus's disappearance. "I really thought he'd turn up by now," Rex finished. "If he'd died, I think they would have found a body. There's a sandbar nearby that blocks the tide, and the water's not that deep. I checked the ways out of town—bus, airplane shuttle services—but no one left who meets Pop's description."

"Maybe he was in disguise. It usually works for you."

Rex glanced at his outfit, then over his shoulder at Judith Hunt. "True." He sighed, thinking of the jaunt he planned to take with Pansy to Castle O'Lannaise.

The locked gate she'd mentioned wasn't nearly as intimidating as she assumed. He'd already checked out the grounds, but the house had surprisingly good security, so he hadn't gone inside. He wished Pansy was free to go before the time they'd named.

"At least you know the explosion was rigged, not a mechanical failure," Truman was saying. "If they've set up a forensics table on the beach, the way you said, then maybe they'll pinpoint the origin of the blast. Anyway, maybe we shouldn't tell Ma. At least not until we get some word on Pop."

"No, we have to tell her. Sully'll back me up on it. We can't lie, Truman, not even to protect her. You wouldn't want somebody doing that to you. How is she, anyway?"

"A mess."

"I'll bet," Rex said, his heart aching. He wished he could be there for her. He felt a flash of temper. How could their father have set out self-centeredly to solve a case? Since Judith Hunt hadn't found any bodies, Rex was even more sure than before that Augustus was alive. Chances were, whoever he'd been with had lived also. "Ma always tries to buck up when she's on the phone with me."

"Well," Truman said, abruptly switching the subject and trying to lighten the mood, "I know one way to cheer her up."

"What's that?"

"Marriage. When it comes to getting our fifteen million, I've done my part."

"You have," Rex agreed. Since their meeting at the Steeles' Greenwich Village home, Rex had learned that Trudy Busey had accepted Truman's proposal of marriage. "How's Sully doing on that score?"

"Better now that Judith Hunt's out of his hair."

"She's definitely hell on wheels," Rex agreed. "You should see her charging around here. What would make a woman so intent on prosecuting other cops?"

Truman ignored the question about the Internal Affairs officer. "C'mon, Rex. What about you? Have you found a wife yet?"

The words were so unexpected that Rex laughed, and then just as quickly he sobered, thinking of the time he'd spent with Pansy Hanley—both as Jacques O'Lannaise and as Ned Nelson. "I'm not sure," he found himself saying, the words coming as a surprise to him. "Maybe."

PANSY'S BODY was feverish, her chest rising and falling, pressing hard into the mattress with every quickening breath. In the dream, Jacques was on top of her, loving her. He'd come to her through the French doors leading onto the stone patio, and after entering her room, he'd left the doors open. Summer air blew inside, blustery and tempestuous with a coming storm, pungent with sea scents and something she couldn't name. Sandalwood? Jasmine?

The air stirred the white curtains around her canopy bed, then the dream broke up, becoming disjointed. Images seemed to shatter, splitting like broken light into filaments. Wouldn't her father hear her and Jacques's lovemaking? she wondered. Wouldn't he realize Jacques had broken into their home? That she was being ravished by a pirate?

But her father was dead. She wasn't Iris Hanley,

was she? she thought in confusion. No, she was Pansy.
Pansy Hanley. Iris was her ancestor.

And yet, somehow Jacques was here. In her bedroom. Strong, dark hands were possessively cupping
her breasts, the fingers curling over flesh. He pinched
and stroked the pebbled peaks, rolling them between
his fingers, making her beg senselessly for things he
was withholding.

But how could that be? In reality, Pansy was lying
on her belly, wasn't she? And something—Jacques's
weight—was pressing her deeper into the soft mattress. That's why she felt so breathless. Suddenly she
realized she wasn't naked, as she'd thought. No, lus-
cious-feeling hands caught the hem of the knee-length
white gown she'd worn to bed, and he slowly glided
the gown upward, caressing her as he did so, exploring the backs of her knees, then her behind, not stopping until he'd removed the gown entirely.

Tossing, she rubbed her face into the pillow, emitting a moan as her parted lips caught on the cotton of
the pillowcase. "Yes," Pansy whispered in sleep, just
as a stream of warm liquid oozed onto her back. Wide-
splayed hands followed, his flattened palms massaging her, grasping her muscles. With the heels of his
hands, he created circular magic. Swirling sensations
pooled right to her already damp core as he rubbed oil
into her skin. Her legs parted slightly.

She felt so relaxed.

So incredibly, blissfully relaxed and aroused.

Almonds. Mixing with the salty air, the scent was
drawn into her lungs as the warmth and strength of
Jacques's exploring hands released the oil's pungence.
Those hands, she thought mindlessly, those glorious

hands, as thumbs bracketed her spine, slipping and sliding from tailbone to midback—up, then down again. Once, twice. And then, on a sweeping downward motion, she instinctively lifted for him as he fluidly dragged her panties down her legs.

She felt a flutter of silk as they traced over her insteps. And then they were gone, and she stretched her arms, hugging the pillow more tightly. "Yes. Oh, yes," she whispered again, her hips seeking as the man began kneading her bottom. That almond air sucked through her teeth as she responded, her hips tilting and rolling, bringing her aching mound to the hard mattress, as if such a silly gesture could really bring the satisfaction she needed from him.

What was he doing to her? she wondered. How did he manage it? Excitement built as a palm slid beneath her, sandwiched between her silken upper thigh and the mattress. As the hand traveled higher, she arched upward, giving him access. When he took it, she gasped, starting to awaken.

All at once, she was too damn hot, about to come. The hand was beneath her, wedged firmly where her thighs joined, tightly squeezing her, and she moved breathlessly against it, knowing she'd never felt anything so good.

"Jacques," she whispered, aware of her breasts, loose and straining. Aching, peaking tips desperately needed the salve of his other hand, to be massaged with the oil, touched by the comforting, soothing warmth of his mouth.

"Too hot," she murmured fitfully. She was burning up. She wanted rid of the covers. A frustrated groan escaped from between her lips, then a needy, annoyed pant. *Take the gown off,* she fretted. Why wouldn't he remove her clothes? What was wrong with this man? Didn't he want her naked? But he had taken it off, hadn't he?

Please...

Another moan burst from her. Deep, it came from somewhere far down in her throat as she ground her body against his waiting hand, a hand curving like a cup that held pure pleasure. She felt his strong knees brace themselves between hers. Widening his stance, he opened her, parted her, then lifted her so that she, too, was on her knees.

That's when she realized she wasn't asleep anymore.

Just as she registered he was no dream phantom and that he was fully naked and sheathed with protection, he pressed inside. She didn't need to turn around. She knew who he was. She recognized the feeling of him, the way he burst through her, stripping her of thought. She wasn't surprised he'd found his way into her bedroom. This man, she was sure, could walk through walls.

The climax was immediate. Intense. Palpitations still rippled through her limbs as he continued taking her, pushing her toward another ecstatic peak. She was breathless, damp with sweat, amazed this man could pull such a response from her. She tried to turn and glimpse his face, but another strong climax forced her to grasp a sheet. It was damp from her perspiration, and she was still clutching it when she felt his release.

A second later, they collapsed, their breathing harsh, their bodies satisfied. She felt him rest atop her back, and she smiled as the sweet curve of his lips buried in her neck. He was kissing damp strands of her hair. She tried to calm herself, to catch her breath, and she waited until she felt his limbs relax completely, until she felt his mouth tilt into a grin against her skin.

That's when she took the advantage. Swiftly, she rolled. Catching him off guard, she turned him onto his back, straddled him, then quickly flicked on the bedside lamp.

Squinted against the light, she stared into his face. Up close, with his face illuminated, he was just as gorgeous as she recalled. His face was chiseled from dusky stone, the cheekbones high, the oval jaw rough and dark. His eyes were the strange gray-green-blue of the ocean in the morning fog, and the expression of them right now was dreamy and unperturbed, as if this was exactly how he'd expected their lovemaking to end. Even worse, he really did look exactly like Jacques O'Lannaise. Pansy stared at him a long moment, trying to ignore the searing gaze he traced over her breasts, and then in a sleep-scratchy voice, she demanded, "Who the hell are you?"

6

HE'D NEVER TOLD HER his name. Pansy knotted a green silk bathrobe three days later, yawning as she entered the kitchen, the limbs of her well-loved body feeling as loose as untied Christmas ribbons. He'd come to her for the past three nights, and every night was better than the last. Still, she was beyond frustrated with herself. Why hadn't she managed to learn more about him? A few nights ago, she'd been straddling him, feeling confident he was right where she wanted him, and then suddenly he'd turned the tables, reversed their positions and trapped her beneath him.

"Must have been some dream," said Lily.

Hardly a dream. Every blessed second of these past few nights had been as real as it gets. Fighting the heated flush rising on her cheeks, Pansy glanced at her sister, who was clad in a bikini from an early morning swim. Seated at the table with a towel draped around her waist, Lily was shoveling down spoonfuls of granola and rapidly jotting on a sheet of expensive notepaper she'd probably gotten as a sample for possible sale in her store.

"Sit," commanded Vi. Two hands settled on Pansy's shoulders and pressed her into a chair. "I'll get your cereal. You look like hell."

"Gee, thanks," said Pansy dryly, sending Vi, who

was dressed for work in her mail carrier's uniform, a long, sideways glance.

"Tousled hell," Lily clarified, eyeing her sister curiously. "What's going on? You've looked like this for days, Pansy. Was there someone here last night we don't know about?"

"You should talk," Pansy returned, her voice hoarse from lack of sleep. "I could swear I heard Lou Fairchild's car roar out of the driveway early this morning."

Lily smirked. "He was gone by midnight, if you must know."

"One," corrected Vi.

"She only knows this," assured Lily, "because Garth Garrison was still here."

Pansy chuckled. "I thought you hated him, Vi."

"I do," returned Vi loftily, "but I intend to get my hands on that lottery money." Her voice hitched with excitement as she continued. "You know, I really do think he won. He's been talking about buying a second home, a condo in Manhattan, and he's pricing sailboats."

"Even without a lottery win, that man's probably loaded," said Lily. "Everybody knows he can afford better than that tumbledown shack he calls home, so that doesn't mean anything. Besides, Lou came right out and informed me that he's got a huge secret he wants to share with me. Huge. That was the word he used. He says he's just not ready to tell me about it yet."

"He's probably afraid to announce he's got the hots for you," said Vi. "Although the rest of us noted the obvious long ago."

"Aren't you observant," Lily returned dryly.

"Very," assured Vi.

Pansy considered telling her sisters neither man had won, but she hated to throw a wet blanket over their manhunt. She hadn't seen her sisters this happy about their prospects for years. Besides, she couldn't prove her point without revealing her indiscreet nighttime trysts with a stranger, something that would turn Lily and Vi into protective mothering hens.

Not that she cared. She sucked in a quick breath, held it a moment, then exhaled slowly as she recalled last night's lovemaking. Who was the man? He seemed so safe and protective. He was conscientious about her comfort and pleasure, too, not to mention respectful. So, why was he insisting on keeping his identity hidden?

To drive me crazy, Pansy thought, a smile tugging at her lips. *And heighten my pleasure.* The truth was, it had turned into sort of a game where she apprised him of whatever research she'd done during the day in an effort to find out who he was. And she would, too. No man could vanish into thin air, as he seemed to do at dawn.

Meantime, Pansy wasn't about to ruin the sumptuous affair by sharing it with her siblings. If they knew, they'd start camping outside her bedroom door, ready to pounce on the man and grill him themselves. Ditto that, if Pansy told them he'd taken the lottery letter from the bulletin board at Zaw's.

She sighed wistfully. Last night, her wealthy suitor had visited again using the French doors, and while, once more, she'd been determined to refuse his love-

An Important Message
from the Editors

Dear Reader,

Because you've chosen to read one of our fine romance novels, we'd like to say "thank you!" And, as a special way to thank you, we've selected two more of the books you love so well, plus an exciting Mystery Gift, to send you absolutely FREE!

Please enjoy them with our compliments...

Pam Powers

P.S. And because we value our customers, we've attached something extra inside...

Peel off seal and Place inside...

How to validate your Editor's
FREE GIFT
"Thank You"

1. Peel off gift seal from front cover. Place it in space provided at right. This automatically entitles you to receive 2 FREE BOOKS and a fabulous mystery gift.

2. Send back this card and you'll get 2 brand-new Harlequin Temptation® novels. These books have a cover price of $3.99 each in the U.S. and $4.50 each in Canada, but they are yours to keep absolutely free.

3. There's no catch. You're under no obligation to buy anything. We charge nothing—ZERO—for your first shipment. And you don't have to make any minimum number of purchases—not even one!

4. The fact is, thousands of readers enjoy receiving their books by mail from the Harlequin Reader Service®. They enjoy the convenience of home delivery...they like getting the best new novels at discount prices BEFORE they're available in stores...and they love their *Heart to Heart* subscriber newsletter featuring author news, horoscopes, recipes, book reviews and much more!

5. We hope that after receiving your free books you'll want to remain a subscriber. But the choice is yours— to continue or cancel, any time at all! So why not take us up on our invitation, with no risk of any kind. You'll be glad you did!

6. Don't forget to detach your FREE BOOKMARK. And remember...just for validating your Editor's Free Gift Offer, we'll send you THREE gifts, *ABSOLUTELY FREE!*

GET A
FREE MYSTERY GIFT...

*SURPRISE MYSTERY GIFT
COULD BE YOURS **FREE** AS
A SPECIAL "THANK YOU" FROM
THE EDITORS OF HARLEQUIN*

Visit us online at
www.eHarlequin.com

making until he offered a name, his silent counterarguments—delivered in wet, wild kisses—had overwhelmed her. She simply couldn't help herself. What healthy woman could?

He'd started the night by slowly, painstakingly undressing her, pushing back the shoulders of her gown just enough so he could lift a breast to the liquid heat of his lips, followed by the languid swirl of his tongue. And then his tongue glided lower, feeling like drenched satin on her skin. Long, hot strokes singed her belly. Feathering touches rimmed and dipped inside her navel, and then in a move that turned her limbs to water, he'd used his tongue to part her cleft. Slowly, gently, with the most cherished care she'd ever experienced, he'd sponged her heated core until she was twisting beneath him, whimpering for more, begging him to take her to completion. Which, of course, he did.

"I think she's got a crush on Ned Nelson," Vi said.

Pansy cued into the conversation, grasping Vi's hand as she set a bowl of granola in front of Pansy. "Oh, no, not soy milk," Pansy murmured. "I wanted the good old-fashioned cow stuff."

"Too late," quipped Vi, liberally splashing Pansy's granola. "If you want killer milk with all those hormones, you'll have to wake up earlier and get your own breakfast."

"The next thing you know," grumbled Pansy, "she'll have us eating seeds for supper."

"Speaking of supper," said Lily, finishing her notes, "I made a list for the cookout. You guys still want to have people over this weekend, right?"

"Right," said Pansy and Vi in unison.

"I figured we could grill hot dogs and burgers and maybe serve that hot potato salad Great-Aunt Celia used to make. The recipe's around here somewhere." Lily lifted an eyebrow. "And no offense, but why are we asking Judith Hunt and the divers she's working with?"

"She's about as personable as an iceberg," agreed Vi. "Not exactly a guest who promises to be the life of the party."

"Ned said he wanted a chance to talk to her," Pansy said, shrugging. "He's kind of a cop groupie."

Vi shook her head. "Ned, huh? He really doesn't seem like your type, Pansy."

She shrugged. "What's my type?"

"Tall, dark and dangerous," said Vi. "At least when it comes to looks."

"Jacques," Lily said simply.

Her sisters sure had her pegged. Pansy's eyes strayed through the screen door, momentarily settling on some white Adirondack chairs anchored in scrub grass near the dunes and then on a well-worn path that led through some brambles to the road. Farther away, the early-morning fog had rolled out to sea, and the white adobe outbuildings of Castle O'Lannaise gleamed under a cerulean sky.

Dammit, where on earth could her lover go during the day? Where could such a gorgeous guy hide on such a small island? He really did seem to vanish. To make matters worse, two more people had reported seeing a man who bore a striking resemblance to Jacques O'Lannaise, and all were saying they recognized him from one of Iris's framed drawings of the pirate that hung in the local Heritage Museum. The museum had been opened by Priscilla Agnes Hanley in the 1890s and was run by the women's club.

"Pansy, if you don't hurry up and eat that cereal, you're going to be late for work," said Lily, shooting another curious glance at her sister. "You're getting as bad as Vi. Are you positive you're not still upset about seeing what happened to that boat?"

"Yes," said Pansy.

And if one more person asked, Pansy felt she'd snap. How could she explain that her world had turned inside out? That she was falling madly, hopelessly in love with a man she didn't even know? That all day, she caught herself daydreaming while showing new properties and greeting incoming vacationers?

The knowledge of the secret affair burned inside her, just as her body burned when her mysterious lover pressed intimately against her, his eyes hot with moonlight and penetrating with passion. But no, she simply couldn't tell her sisters, as much as she'd like for someone to know about this, just in case...

Something happens to me. She pushed away the barely conscious thought, not wanting to examine her tiny niggling doubts about him. Anyway, her sisters would insist she not meet with him again. Or demand to accompany her, so they could find out who he was. Even worse, they'd voice concern that he might be dangerous.

Which he couldn't be, not given how good he felt in her arms and how sweetly he spooned against her when they slept—his smile tracing her bare shoulder, his torso molding to her back. Once satisfied, the man was as snuggly as a kitten.

"You are running late," put in Vi. "And it's not like you."

"Pansy's not acting like herself," agreed Lily, as if Pansy wasn't even there.

"I, Pansy Hanley," vowed Pansy, lifting a hand solemnly, "am fine."

"Good. That means you'll be free after work to shop for the cookout," said Lily, turning her eyes to the grocery list.

Pansy slapped the heel of her palm to her forehead. "Sorry," she said, emitting a sound of frustration over her forgetfulness. "I can't go today. I'm meeting Ned after work."

Vi shot Pansy a pointed look. "While your sisters are slaving away, preparing for the cookout you requested? Your sisters," Vi added, "who also could have had hot dates."

"It's not a date," defended Pansy, trying to ignore the sudden, surprising stab of disloyalty she felt toward Ned. "Ned and I are just friends." Although Pansy was beginning to suspect Ned wanted more. Vaguely, she wondered how she'd feel about him if she wasn't having an illicit affair that was so thoroughly out of character for her.

Vi still looked peeved. "Where are you going?"

Pansy couldn't believe she'd forgotten. Chalk it up to feeling blissfully foggy after a night of the world's most exquisite lovemaking. "Castle O'Lannaise."

There was a very long silence. And then Lily and Vi groaned.

"I CAN SEE why you needed the security," Ned said, disgust tingeing his tone as he used the toe of a sneaker to brush aside some dust on the parquet floor.

Outside, a round, red sun was dropping over the horizon, and the last rays of the day's rose-touched twilight streamed through narrow, floor-to-ceiling windows. Shoving her hands into the back pockets of the jeans she'd worn with a T-shirt and sandals, Pansy followed Ned's gaze around the spacious drawing room of the main house. In the growing darkness, beer bottles were visible through a plastic trash bag, and half-burned nubs of candles could be seen, cemented by their wax to a skirt of gray stones surrounding the fireplace. Dust was caked on a window seat.

"At least there's no graffiti," Ned said.

"A travesty, isn't it?" Pansy murmured angrily, having realized Ned would sympathize over the disrepair. Given that he was an architect, she should have guessed before their arrival that he'd share her love, not to mention her vision, for this once glorious resort. During the hours they'd walked the grounds—taking in everything from the breeding lodge to the watchtower balcony, from the cloistered patio to the countless rooms of the main house—Ned had offered her a wealth of knowledge about resorts built during this era.

As Pansy had detailed her plans for refurbishing, he'd added his own ideas, and the evening had turned into a delightful brainstorming session. Reality had vanished; time had flown. As ideas tumbled out and excitement built, it felt to Pansy as if she and Ned really had the millions it would take to transform the adobe complex.

She wished they did. Maybe she'd broach the subject with her mystery man. She couldn't wait to show Iris's drawings to Ned, both of the estate and of Jacques O'Lannaise, something she'd be able to do soon, since Ned had accepted the invitation to the cookout. Only now did Pansy realize that she hadn't thought of her mystery lover for hours. Funny, she mused. It was almost a blessing to have the obsession lift. For days, all she'd thought about was him, him and him.

Realistically, could a woman love a man she didn't even know? Didn't true love only grow out of sharing and trust? Oh, she'd started living for her sensually charged meetings with the man, but her time with Ned, while less intense, was more pleasant. Or, at least, pleasant in a different way. Less rooted in fantasy, this relationship was starting to feel comfortable, easy, fun.

Sighing, she told herself to quit comparing the men. Her time with each was apples and oranges. Two completely different orders of experience. She surveyed the damage in the room. "A caretaker used to tend the grounds. He lived in the cottage I showed you, near the stables, but whoever owns the place decided paying him was too much of an expenditure."

"So, it's been vacant?"

She nodded. "For a long time now. Kids broke in. It was easy, since the estate's sprawling and isolated. Supposedly haunted, too," she added with a smile. "Ghosts are always a draw."

"You seem to like them," Ned quipped. Something in his expression deepened, and he lowered his voice. "Did you find whatever you meant to this evening, Pansy?"

She shrugged, unsure. "I...just kept thinking I saw shadows in the windows."

"But you didn't?"

"Guess not." She returned his smile. "Anyway," she continued, returning to their earlier subject, "I tried to clean up after the kids. I left the last trash bag in case I needed it."

"I'll be glad to help do whatever you need to around here."

"Thanks. I might take you up on it. I did finally get the go-ahead to install better security. Since then, no one's been inside." She paused. "At least not to my knowledge."

Ned shook his head. "It's a shame. People should enjoy a wonder like this. Structurally, the buildings are in great shape. Amazing, really," he added, "when you consider how long the place has been vacant."

"Wouldn't it make the perfect honeymoon resort?" She couldn't help but ask, her heart swelling with the romance of the idea. "Can't you just see it? Outdoors, the fountains would be working, the water illuminated by colored floodlights."

"Maybe you could change the colors. You know, the way they do at the Empire State Building."

"Great idea," she enthused, picking up the thread. "Red and green on Christmas, pink on Valentine's day."

"Don't forget. You'll need horses, too."

She sighed wistfully, imagining thoroughbreds and Arabians stamping their hooves in the stables. She could almost smell the scents of hay and grain mixing with the salty breeze. "I'm sure the guests would love to ride."

"You really think people would visit?"

"'If you build it, they will come,'" she returned philosophically, adapting the famous line from the movie *Field of Dreams*.

Ned shot her a teasing smile. "I hate to mention it, but your island is cursed. Which means it's got a bad reputation for nasty storms and hurricanes."

She nodded. "Yeah. Unfortunately, there are rumblings we might get a storm next week." She shrugged. "But you visited, didn't you?"

He chuckled. "You got me there."

It was impossible not to smile back. In the dimming light, Ned looked boyishly exuberant, as energized by their outing as she. As usual, his overlong blond shaggy bangs made her itch to find scissors and give him a trim, and the shirt hanging loosely over his khakis needed the business end of an iron. Colorwise, however, today's shirt was uncharacteristically tame, sporting red-and-white stripes and navy patch pockets printed with white stars.

He tilted his head, and eyes that customarily twinkled good-naturedly had sharpened. "What?" she whispered, squinting with concern.

"The back door," he mouthed. "I heard someone."

Her mind raced. Had they left the door open when they came in? Or had someone been inside the house all along? If so, how had they breached the security? And was the person responsible for the shadows Pansy had seen in the windows?

Lifting a finger to indicate she should stay put— which she wouldn't, of course—Ned edged around an arch into the hallway, his movements so stealthy he could have been a professional tracker. Pansy followed, narrowing her eyes. No light intruded here, and Pansy peered down what looked like a long, narrow tunnel.

A shadow moved near a staircase! The sharp sound of her surprised inhalation startled her, and she nearly leaped out of her skin. But it was only Ned. He'd almost reached the back door already. How did he get that far? Just as she pressed a calming hand to her heart, he took off, sprinting, and since he was apparently no longer worried about making noise, Pansy lunged after him. By the time she reached the screen door, it was swinging toward her. She caught it, pushed through it, then pounded across a patio into the grass.

"Ned?" she called, wishing the last rays of light weren't vanishing. Overhead, the clouds seemed to dance across the sky, shifting into eerie shapes. She peered into the darkness and continued running. She shouted, "Are you okay?"

Where was he? "Dammit," she whispered, panic racing through her as she glanced around. Ned wasn't the kind of guy who should be chasing people. "Come back," she said. "We'll call the police." Surely Judith Hunt or one of the local men could take care of this.

Pansy gasped. Ned wasn't alone! Up ahead, moving toward a stand of tall trees, Ned's shadowy figure was darting into the ever-deepening darkness. Another figure—a man—was in front of him, dodging left then right, trying to evade the swinging arc of Ned's arm. She thought she heard Ned curse as he swiped the air, trying to grasp the back of the man's clothes.

"Leave him alone," Pansy repeated, lifting her voice. "Come back and we'll call the police."

She watched with horror as Ned lunged—and missed! How had it happened? she wondered a second later, gaping. He'd been so close. Pansy wasn't ten feet away. But when Ned reached for the intruder, his hand had seemed to move right through the man.

As if he was a ghost. Shuddering involuntarily, she blinked. The intruder had vanished. But where had he gone? If he'd run into the stand of trees, why hadn't she heard him?

There was no time to wonder. Ned had fallen to his knees. Pansy speeded her steps, ignoring the air knifing to her lungs and the sharp pain in her side. Dropping down beside Ned, she grasped his shoulders, barely aware that her hands began roving over him as if she was a new mother exploring her baby.

"Are you all right?"

He shook his head in disgust, rising to his feet and dusting off his pants. "I missed him."

"It's okay," she commiserated, hoping his male ego wasn't too injured.

His lips pursed into a grim line. "I almost had him."

"You sure did," she said in her best cheerleader tone. Since Ned looked fine, she added, "Did you get a look at him?"

"Six feet. Dark, closely cropped hair, dark eyes."

Half listening, she realized she was concentrating hard on Ned's breathing, which was still labored. Why was it stirring memories her mind couldn't quite capture? She felt the same hazy feeling of dislocation that swept over her whenever she thought of her mystery lover, and although she tried, she couldn't shake off the feeling.

And then suddenly, she registered four things at

once: Ned's breathing—the sharp catch of it and the
quick way he exhaled—sounded like her night lover's.
Second, the description of the man he'd nearly caught
matched her night lover's. Third, Ned Nelson had
been far, far quicker on his feet than she'd have expected. And fourth, when he'd given the description
of the man he'd been chasing, Ned Nelson had
sounded like a cop. She pushed aside the thoughts,
but she realized Ned was definitely sharper than he
appeared.

7

A FEW NIGHTS LATER, as Pansy stepped lightly through a screen door and onto the porch where Ned was waiting for her, she paused long enough to pull in a deep, heady breath. Truly, she thought, there was nothing like the scent of the sea. She could smell charcoal and burgers from the cookout, too, and from the back of the house came the shouts of guests who were still playing volleyball.

She smiled. "Sounds like they're having a good time, huh?"

"Would you like to join them?" Ned asked.

The truth was, she hadn't really dressed for it. Shaking her head, she adjusted her grip on the black artist's portfolio she was carrying, then she withdrew Iris and Jacques's letters from a pocket of her sundress. There were only a handful—seven exactly—tied together with a dusty, velvet faded-red ribbon.

Realizing Ned was watching her intently, Pansy felt strangely conscious of the dress she'd chosen. It was delicate, one of her favorites, made of sky-blue silk. Lighter than air, it swished across her knees when she walked, making soft, enticing whispering sounds. Since it had an underskirt and was sheer, she was wearing nothing beneath but a thong, and right about now—maybe because of the after-dinner brandy she and Ned had been drinking—she was enjoying the decidedly delicious feel of air circulating under her skirt and tickling her bottom.

Of course, the stifling heat, not Ned, had motivated her to wear such a sexy wisp of a dress, she told herself. For the same reason, she'd brushed her hair loosely upward, wrapping the honey strands into a complicated knot she'd decorated with sprigs of baby's breath. Tendrils clung to her neck, which was slightly damp from perspiration, but at least that left her skin bare to the breeze, and the silk neckline was comfortably low, ending just when her breasts began to spill out of it. The bodice was held firmly in place by straps fashioned from tiny white ceramic beads.

"It's hot," she complained, suddenly afraid he'd think she'd worn the dress for him. After all, most people at the cookout had worn shorts and T-shirts, including Judith Hunt, who usually wore suits even while working on the beach. Before Ned could respond, Pansy's smile broadened, and she cast a maternal glance at him. Just as Ned had hoped, he'd been able to talk shop with the female officer much of the night, and Pansy was glad. Listening to Ned ply the woman with questions, an unknowing passerby might have mistaken him, not Judith, for the law enforcement official.

He shrugged lazily. "It's supposed to be hot. It's summer. Are you coming out or are you just going to stand there?" Swirling amber brandy in a squat snifter, he surveyed her from a porch swing her father had built and hung years ago.

"Coming out," she said, even though she didn't move.

"What's got you so pensive?"

She glanced fleetingly toward Castle O'Lannaise. It had been a few days since their encounter with the intruder, but she was still plagued by the odd sensations she'd felt after Ned gave chase. The thought was crazy, but briefly, for less than a heartbeat, something about Ned had reminded her of her mystery man. She couldn't stop mulling over how the intruder had slipped through Ned's fingers. He'd seemed to vanish into thin air.

Pushing away the thoughts, she managed a shrug. "It's shaping up to be a very strange summer," she finally offered.

"How so?"

Because night after night, a sexy stranger was coming into her bedroom, touching her body in a way she'd never imagined a man could. Even more surprising, she—who was usually much more circumspect—was letting him. Beyond that, she was creating a relationship with Ned that felt as comfortable as that which she'd previously only shared with girlfriends. "Oh, I don't know," she murmured. "But you've never been down to the Heritage Museum," she continued, her tone teasing and her words trailing off as she let the screen door swing shut behind her.

"I'm going to," Ned defended. "And I'm going to take the Hanley sisters' tour."

"So you say," Pansy chided, tucking her skirt beneath her as she took a seat on the swing next to Ned and opened the portfolio. Her heart skipped a beat as she peered inside. The drawings were old, but they'd been carefully stored, as had Iris's letters, so they were well-preserved. Pansy had looked at the sketches so many times she'd nearly memorized each stroke left by Iris's hand—the dark, thickly etched brows, the tiny lines around Jacques's glinting eyes, the careful shading that hollowed his cheeks, making his face appear almost gaunt.

"Jacques O'Lannaise," she pronounced. Rather than turning the picture around, she continued gazing at the pirate's visage with mixed emotions, her eyes settling on a wedge of dark hair that pointed, like an arrow, toward the center of his unusually high forehead. The rest of his hair was thrust back, and the strands lay in visible furrows, as if the man had just rifled his fingers through them.

The eyes were utterly captivating. This was only a drawing, but if she hung it on a wall, the eyes would follow her wherever she went. Even now, it didn't seem possible, but the man who came to her each night looked exactly like this. The resemblance was remarkable. Uncanny. Every time she thought of these sketches, there seemed only one explanation for the appearance of her dream lover—that he really was a ghost.

And yet what he did to her body was sinfully real. Could a picture come to life? It certainly seemed so. As she thought of the previous night, her nipples hardened, aching as they beaded against the sumptuous, barely there silk. Her lover had been so commanding, his hands almost rough as they explored every inch of her body. All day, she'd been remembering their open-palmed strength as he'd wrapped his arms around her bare back and used those hands to pull her closer, arching his hips as he did so, pushing himself completely inside her.

Dawn had some so soon. She'd begged him to stay,

but apparently she'd drifted to sleep. When she'd awakened he was gone. It wasn't a mistake she'd make again. No, tonight she was going to follow him home. Meantime, traitorous memories were sending heat prancing through her veins, and while she told herself she simply couldn't make love to him again— not one more time—without knowing more about him, she also knew she couldn't wait for his return.

Blushing, sucking in a quick breath when she glanced down and saw how obviously she was affected, Pansy shifted away from Ned and lifted her brandy glass.

His tone was playful, his eyes warm in a way that made her feel sure he hadn't missed her arousal. "Aren't you going to show me your fantasy man?"

She wanted to deny that soft, teasing taunt. "He's not my fantasy man," she defended, striving for a playful tone to match Ned's, even though she knew he could probably read the naked emotions in her eyes. How could it be otherwise, when she was gazing into the face of a man who was loving her so well?

"Something tells me you're lying."

"Maybe." The alcohol, meant to diffuse a flood of sensations, had only served to further warm her. She wasn't usually a drinker, and as she tipped the glass for another sip, she shuddered. Liquid hit the back of her throat, then slid slowly downward, burning in her belly. It felt hot, dark and forbidden, like the stranger's kisses, and it fired dangerous sparks into her blood, filling her with something devilish and daring she'd never known was inside her until this crazy summer. Maybe she should know better than to follow the call of the man's passion, but didn't every

woman crave the experience of wild, abandoned loving—just once?

Unexpectedly, she throbbed. The swift, sudden
pressure and slow burning ache between her legs
were truly uncomfortable, more than she could bear.
She realized Ned was watching her intently. He'd
seemed to register the changes in her body, and the
moment was suddenly charged, the already hot summer air becoming that much hotter.

"So, you want to see my fantasy man?" she murmured. Slowly, she turned the picture so he could see.

Ned, who'd been lounging with his hands thrust
deep into the pockets of his khakis, slowly set his
brandy on the swing's armrest and simply stared.

"What?" asked Pansy, her voice catching throatily.
Why couldn't Ned tear his eyes from the image?
"Uh...you look like you've seen a ghost," she ven-
tured, but the joke fell flat.

With difficulty, Ned pulled his gaze away from the
pirate's picture. "Iris's sketch is just...so good," he replied, but his tone was strained, and she was sure he
was lying. But why? And why was he looking at
Jacques O'Lannaise as if he'd seen him before? "Sure
you haven't experienced a sighting?" she suggested.
"Like that kid Harlin Gills?"

Ned chuckled, but the laughter didn't reach his
eyes. "Hardly. If I see your ghost, you'll be the first to
know."

"Then why such a strong reaction to the picture?"

She never found out. Ned shrugged and scooted
closer, his weight feeling warm and familiar against
her as he began leafing through the sketches, talking
about each in turn, clearly impressed by Iris's talent

with charcoal and chalk. Only much later, when they'd begun to read Iris and Jacques's letters, did she catch Ned's gaze returning to the open portfolio—and the picture of Jacques O'Lannaise.

"What?" she asked again.

He shook his head. "Just admiring the stationery," he lied, looking at a sheet in his hand. It was heavy, the color of rich cream, and the bold, masculine strokes of Jacques's calligraphy, visible after so many years, had barely faded, making the letter look as if it had been written yesterday.

"Lily still carries the paper in her store," Pansy said conversationally. "It's from a Parisian vendor who's been manufacturing it since the mid seventeen hundreds."

"Beautiful," Ned murmured, rubbing the expensive stock between the thumb and forefinger of his artistic hands.

Ned looked as if he, too, were under the spell of Jacques and Iris. Watching him, Pansy had to fight the sudden impulse to confide about her dream lover. It was a harebrained notion. But what if he was a ghost? Or someone disguising himself as Jacques O'Lannaise? But then, she wondered, why would someone want to do that? Except to seduce her, she thought. Did someone care for her enough to discover and fullfil her deepest fantasy?

She took a deep breath, deciding she couldn't say anything. She had no idea what Ned would do with such a confession, but she supposed he might be a bit jealous. And yet, first and foremost, he was her friend, wasn't he? Because of the time they'd spent together, she trusted him. And she was sure he'd accept her unconditionally.

"I've always wanted to take them to a handwriting expert," she said, pulling her attention to the letters.

"Great idea," he returned. Using a finger, he pushed his black-framed glasses up the bridge of his nose, then squinted as he surveyed Jacques's writing. "What insights do you think an analysis would give as to his character?"

She considered. "The analyst would say he was...strong. Mysterious. Secretive," she added, although she wasn't thinking of Jacques, but of her lover.

For a long moment, they fell silent, and although a light was on, dark clouds passed overhead, turning the porch darker. He offered, "I think they're right about a storm coming, but it's a nice night."

Romantic, too, Pansy thought, glancing into bushes that blinked with fireflies. Just on the other side of some dunes, the surf was dragging shells across the sand. The horn of a tugboat sounded. Unbidden, she caught herself wondering if Ned had really sensed the desire thrumming through her as she'd looked at Jacques's pictures. Had Ned noticed her breasts peaking? The desire she'd tried so hard to hide?

She was sure of it, then surer still as he began to read Jacques's last letter to Iris. Ned squinted in the darkness, his voice low, throaty and for a brief second—nothing more than the blink of an eye—oddly familiar.

The water's rising, my dearest. The mighty ocean's currents swell ever higher onto the land.

Far below me, a humble cottage was swept to sea; wrenched from its roots by furious tides, it swirled away, spinning into a deluge of salt spray and dark mist.

Perched so far above danger, I can almost touch the clouds that dance madly in the air above the castle I've built for you, the castle you've vowed to share with me, my love.

Or was that a lie? Have you left me, darling? Have you stopped being able to fight your father's plans to part us? My messenger says no one's accepted my letters. Where have you gone? Why aren't you here?

I've just come from the storm, but I saw you nowhere! My heart is breaking. It's this night we were to run away together! You're to be mine! And I won't—I can't!—leave this island until I hear you speak your love for me again.

When I stare into the turbulent sky, fear shudders through me. I am praying for your safety, Iris, ready to curse this hellish island if you vanish. Wind slashes hard rains against the windows, my darling. A cloud shaped as a horse-drawn carriage races across the mad, tempestuous sky, and my only hope is that it might bear you to me. Without you, I'll perish.

Ned's low, steady voice had lured her nearer like a lullaby. Inch by inch, Pansy had been drawn closer as he read, and she realized she'd come too close. Ned's lips were only a whisper away, and his breath was so near she caught the scent and heat of brandy.

Aware of her, his eyes widened behind the dark-framed glasses, and his gaze locked to hers. "Pansy," he murmured, leaning a fraction, his lips gently sweeping her cheek. The light touch shouldn't have jarred her, but it sent her senses reeling. *There's more to him,* she thought in an inexplicable, vague panic. *More to Ned.* In stunned surprise, she leaned away, hoping to still her suddenly hammering heart. What was going on? she wondered in total shock. Without her knowing it, had she begun to have sensual feelings for Ned? It was as if they'd surreptitiously slipped under the skirt of her consciousness.

Too late, she registered his look of dismay. It didn't last. Like a phantom, it vanished from his features almost instantly, and he smiled. "Sorry," he murmured, apologizing for the kiss.

"No," she said, feeling baffled by her response to him, the one word she spoke just a whisper on the sultry breeze. "I..."

But it was too late. He didn't let her finish. Instead, he lifted a forefinger and pressed it to her lips. "Shh. You don't need to explain."

But she did, if only to herself. For weeks, she'd been getting to know Ned while simultaneously having one of the world's strangest affairs. Was she confusing growing feelings for Ned with those for a man who was carrying her nightly to oblivion? One man was loving her body, the other her mind. And didn't she need both kinds of love?

Wistful sadness twisted inside her. She needed to discover the stranger's identity. She had to know if there was any future in the passion they shared. Which was more important to her—the understanding Ned offered? Or the unprecedented, dark emotion conjured by her lover's touches?

"I'd better be going, Pansy," Ned said gently.

Looking at him, she wondered if this was goodbye. He'd approached her as a friend, but apparently he'd come to feel more. "I'll see you tomorrow night?" she asked, her voice hitching with emotion she didn't try to suppress.

"Maybe before," he murmured, rising to go.

Relief flooded her, surprising her with its intensity, and she squinted at him hopefully. "Before?"

As if realizing what he'd said, he thought a long moment, then clarified. "Maybe I'll stop by the realty office so we can have lunch."

Lunch.

She'd never imagined such a mundane word could make her feel so good. Whatever his feelings for her, Ned Nelson wasn't giving up—at least not yet.

HE HAD NO RIGHT to be furious, Rex reminded himself, his sandaled feet sinking into the soft sand as he circled the porch where he'd sat with Pansy only hours before. After all, this was a situation of his own making, wasn't it?

Frustrated, he shook his head. Absently scratching his chest—he'd worn a blousy, white button-down shirt open over his jeans—he wondered how things had gotten so tangled. At first, he hadn't trusted Pansy not to tell Judith Hunt who he was, and if Judith found out now, she'd prosecute him for the deception in addition to ending his search for Augustus.

Now he had to face the truth. At this point, he could probably trust Pansy, but he'd come to hope she'd choose Ned. After all, that's who Rex really was, wasn't he? Not in name, but personality. Hadn't Pansy been stunned by their compatibility that day at Castle O'Lannaise? he thought angrily. Or by the visions they'd shared for refurbishing her castle? Not to mention how Jacques's and Iris's love letters had suffused them both with romance this evening.

His lips pursing, he tried not to dwell on the fiery passion in her gaze as she'd stared at the sketch of Jacques. Nothing more than a glance had made her body respond. He cursed softly, understanding. He'd been shocked to the point of speechlessness when he'd seen the resemblance between himself and her pirate. It was more than striking. It was uncanny.

Lightly, he stepped onto the patio, his heart missing a beat when he saw she'd left the French doors open for him. Swallowing against the sudden dryness of his mouth, he felt a lump lodge in his throat. He thought of her inside—naked, hot and ready beneath the sheets. Eyeing the doors, he wanted to turn and leave, but he knew he couldn't.

Silently, he damned his flesh for its weakness, for the explosion of raw passion she engendered in him that he simply couldn't deny. In his mind, he saw her as she'd been on the porch—standing in a wedge of strong light that shone behind her, illuminating her curves.

Rex had forced himself to look away as if he really was Ned Nelson, which was crazy, since he'd already done so much more than just look. Later, when he'd offered that foolishly chaste kiss, she'd startled and jerked away as if burned. That, too, he thought dryly, was ludicrous, as if his tongue hadn't already been deep inside her mouth—tempting, teasing, exploring...

Thinking of her rejection, he felt an urge...not to punish her, exactly. No, nothing so harsh. Only to keep her waiting, wondering if she'd ever see him again. It wasn't him she wanted anyway, he thought, a scowl overtaking his features. Pansy Hanley wanted a phantom. A ghost. A fantastical figment of her imagination created by a handful of old drawings.

Turn around and go back to Casa Eldora, he schooled himself. But sex with her had left him weak as a baby. He moved toward the doors, slipped inside and silently crossed her bedroom. As he reached for her, one of the ridiculously romantic white curtains surrounding the canopy fluttered outward, tracing his cheek, feeling as soft as her finger.

Yearning unfurled inside him, bringing the insufferable, undeniable arousal he associated with every moment spent in her company. He sought her then. As soon as flesh touched flesh—the back of his hand to her arm—a charged current raced up his sleeve. Almost magically, the air turned thicker, heavier. Electricity sparked. Lust was palpable.

And then she yanked the bubble cord to the bedside lamp.

Taken by surprise, he blinked against the glow. "Ah, *chèrie,*" he murmured, quickly recovering and staring levelly at Pansy, seated primly on the bed, fully dressed in jeans and a T-shirt, her back pressed to the middle of the headboard. "So, you've been waiting for me in the darkness, eh?"

She stared at him evenly, her sea-green eyes as he'd never seen them before—hyperfocused and implacable. Clearly, she'd felt him in the room, stirring the air, before she'd switched on the lamp. She was fully alert. "Game's over." She hugged a pillow to her chest as if in protection. "Who are you?"

When he didn't react to the demanding tone, annoyance claimed her features. She didn't much like that he was still standing, he realized, towering above her in the dim light of the dainty room. He wondered how she'd look if she was aware of the turmoil inside him. Hadn't she guessed that nothing more than her fresh-scrubbed face and her tousled honey hair cascading around her shoulders were enough to make him beg for her?

He bit back a sigh. She'd meant to turn the tables and take him by surprise, and she thought she'd failed. Didn't she know that the very fact of her existence had surprised him more than anything else ever had?

He almost smiled then, even though his frustration was approaching the breaking point. Lowering a hand, he trailed it down the silken tan skin of her cheek. "Hoping to catch me off guard, eh?" he murmured, unable to help the gentle chiding taunt. "Been waiting long?"

She glared at him, the gorgeous lips he'd come here to kiss pressed into a grim little line.

Pushing aside the tail of his shirt, he seated himself next to her on the edge of the bed, somehow glad to see she wasn't as controlled and unaffected as she wanted to appear, at least not given how her eyes trailed to the thick pelt of swirling hair coating his chest, then dropped to his navel, then to the waistband of old, wide-legged jeans, ones so well worn that the denim was smooth with a silken sheen. Heat suffused her cheeks when she saw how lovingly, how gently the denim cupped him.

Suddenly, she edged away—as if only now remembering she was perturbed with him. Scooting across the mattress, she slipped over the side, then dashed for the doors. Instinct propelled him. On his feet in a flash, he gave chase, catching her from behind, his hand circling her wrist.

She'd almost made it across the threshold to the patio, and when she whirled to glare at him, moonlight caught in her hair, making his fingers itch to caress the strands. "I'm not in the mood," Pansy muttered, pressing her back against the doorjamb and crossing her arms over her chest in a way that only served to accentuate full breasts.

Everything about her—her high color, the flashing danger in her green eyes—bespoke passion. "You look very much in the mood," he murmured in correction, pushing nearer, his hand drifting downward until his fingers found and threaded through hers.

"I've got a headache," she assured him.

His eyes twinkled. "Ah. Good thing I'm here. I'm good with headaches."

"Good at causing them," she retorted, stoically staring while his hand—one he suspected felt wonderfully warm—crept around the back of her neck and began kneading her skin. Her lips parted in protest, but her angry eyes betrayed her. They glazed in response, the pupils dilating.

Not that he'd fault her lack of conviction. They were amazing together. Driven by desire, he inched closer, and because he'd stiffened with arousal, the firm bulk curved against her mound. A soft, panting breath sounded, and when he glanced down, he saw that her nipples were erect beneath her shirt.

As if forcibly snapping to attention, her eyes focused once more. "This—" her eyes darted around the room as if searching for a word "—affair we're having..."

"Is wonderful," he finished, his voice hushed with need as he feathered kisses against her cheek. He felt her knees weaken.

"Crazy," she corrected, turning languid in his arms.

When he caught his breath, the scent of her knifed to his lungs. He could smell the rising storm, too, when a blustery current billowed past, lifting the white airy curtains around the bed. The words were out before he knew what he was saying. "I'm falling in love with you."

It wasn't exactly the truth, he realized, gazing at a neck she'd tilted in an invitation his mouth gladly took. The truth was, he wasn't falling. He was already in deep. Angling his head, he nibbled down the slender column of neck, then long strokes of his tongue dampened the bare skin. He blew across the wetness until she shivered.

She whispered, "You can't love someone you don't know."

"I know you." Better than she suspected. *So tell her,* his mind screamed. And yet, if he did, he felt he'd never know the truth about her. His mind hazed with need, but somewhere in the back of it, his childhood ghosted. His father was urging him to be a cop, and he was capitulating because he feared losing his father's love. Pansy, too, seemed to be choosing his darker side over the soul that thrived on romance.

He hated her for it. But there was nothing he could do. She was beginning to writhe. Her seeking hips were tilting upward, straining to meet his jutting arousal, and the explosive pressure nearly sent them both over the edge. Her whimper was barely audible, coming on a jagged pant as he grasped the hem of her shirt and tugged it over her head in a swift movement. Like hell she hadn't intended to make love tonight, he thought.

Her breasts were full, but the brilliant green bra was of a design calculated to lift them and deepen cleavage. "Admit it, *chèrie*," he encouraged hoarsely, leaning so the heated trail of his tongue could trace the bra's lacy border, then flicker inside and touch a still-covered nipple. "No woman wears this if she doesn't expect a man. You've been waiting for me all night because you've been waiting for this."

Her pebbled nipples looked painful, and feeling merciful, he unhooked the bra. Released, she spilled out, tumbling magnificently into his hands. Unable to tear his eyes away, he slid the straps downward, and then he slowly kissed her breasts, each in turn. She shivered—her teeth clacking, a breath whistling between her lips—as he leaned back, his hot gaze roving over her swollen flesh.

"Maybe I was waiting," Pansy admitted throatily, "but I'm determined this time to find out who you are. I'm determined—"

"I'm determined, too," he assured, his searing eyes tracing her chest.

"You don't know me—" The protest was stifled,

lost to the night as he took an aching nipple deeper into his mouth and suckled.

"I know you," he corrected raggedly, groaning when he felt her capitulating hands on his belt, and once more when he heard the metallic rattle of the buckle falling open.

"I know you like to be kissed here. And here," he added, locking his gasping mouth around the other tight peak as she caught his zipper and dragged it over a bursting erection. "Oh, no," he teased, "you've got a headache."

"Not that you care."

"I'd never force myself on a woman," he replied.

"You don't have to," she returned in a rush, as if there was no stopping the flood of her body's begging desire. As he pushed her jeans over her hips, his eyes registered the green panties—cut high, with a narrow strip of silk that barely covered her. He pushed down the panties, too, registering the feverish dampness of her thighs. Just as she kicked away her clothes, his arrowing fingers raced down, gliding over her, dipping inside her for honey.

"I know your desires, Pansy, your dreams."

She was breathless from his touch. "Maybe I know yours." Her hands fell to him then, thrusting inside the open V of his slacks, gliding around his swollen, engorged length. Gently, she gloved him, squeezing—and his mouth slammed down. He kissed her hard.

"You don't know mine," she said, dragging her lips away. "You can't. Not unless you know me. Who are you?"

"You want your castle—" His voice was low. "And you know I can buy it for you." She was boiling, hot and about to crest over, wild with want. Her breasts, the constricted tips still wet and shiny from his mouth, were heaving as she twisted against him, silently begging for release.

He'd trapped her against the door, and since she was free of her jeans, he shed his, readied himself with a condom he'd brought. Then he lifted her, the hard-muscled strength of his arms enough to brace them both.

"C'mon, *chérie*," he murmured, his hands settling on her hips, gripping her, helping her to rise and fall so she could ride him as he walked unsteadily toward the waiting bed. "Let's lie together. Let's share some love, and then some dreams."

She was lost, abandoned to their pleasure, when he lowered her to the bed, pushed deep inside to completely fill her and said, "You want the castle, don't you?"

"Yes," Pansy cried senselessly.

"Then you'll have to do one thing." He was blind with need, barely aware of what he was saying.

"Anything..." She arched to meet him. "Anything."

"Marry me, *chérie*."

Even as he spoke, the words stunned him.

Even more shocking was her reply, a soft, hungry cry. "Yes! Yes! Yes!"

MARRIAGE?

What had she agreed to in the heat of passion? She didn't even know this man! Nevertheless, she'd let him lead her to the bed, suffused once more by hopeless romance and sinful sex. How could she fight that? She was a mere woman! She wasn't a saint! The light was out, but the moon sent a yellow shaft through the open French doors. Staring outside as he slept curled against her, Pansy watched some gray storm clouds break apart and drift across the moon's face, looking like tattered cloth. The night was eerie, and she could taste the increasing moisture in the air, making her wonder when the rains would begin to fall.

She began to drift, then blinked, determined to stay awake. Soon, he'd awaken and slip soundlessly from the bed. His steps, she knew from experience, were as quiet as a ghost's. But she'd hear him. And tonight, she was going to follow him.

Tonight, she was going to demand some answers.

8

LAST NIGHT, her pirate had gone to the last place Pansy expected—Casa Eldora. Which was why she hadn't confronted him and why, this afternoon, she intended to launch a more detailed investigation. Lifting her hand, she rapped on the front door of the cottage, and when no one answered, she knocked again, harder. "No one's home," she whispered.

Flushing guiltily, she glanced over her shoulder toward where she'd parked her car a few doors down, just in case Ned returned, not to mention her lover, and then Pansy fished in her shoulder bag and withdrew the spare key. *Turn around*, a voice inside her urged. *You're not here on official business, which makes this breaking and entering.*

She hesitated, thrusting out her lower lip and blowing upward, trying to cool her face. It didn't help. The day was sweltering and humid, the sky gray. By the time she'd arrived at work this morning, the lavender silk dress she'd chosen was rumpled and drenched with sweat, and now—at half past five—she looked as if she'd spent half the day in a sauna and the other half in a blender.

Jiggling the key into the lock, she sent a troubled glance heavenward. Storm clouds had continued to gather, and because jagged fingers of lightning had been crackling in the sky with increasing frequency, no one was in the water. The weather service was offering advisories, but no rain had fallen. Apparently, Judith Hunt had asked her men to heed the warnings, since they were nowhere in sight.

"Good." Pansy had been worried about having law officers for an audience. Swallowing hard, she shot another uncertain look toward her car. She'd spied on Casa Eldora until Ned left, probably for the Heritage Museum. He'd promised to take advantage of tonight's extended hours.

Taking a deep breath, she pushed open the door. Blessed air-conditioning hit her in a blast. Because she'd rented the cottage to vacationers countless times, she knew it like the back of her hand. Quickly, she glanced around, just in case someone was home. "Hello?" she called.

No answer.

She saw that Ned Nelson's presence hadn't made much of an impression on the place, at least not in the living room, and she recalled that he'd arrived with only two suitcases. She hurriedly entered, then closed the door behind her and began to explore. Pausing at the bathroom, she studied the clean white tiles and dark-striped shower curtain before peering inside the cabinets. Nothing out of the ordinary, she thought, then proceeded to rifle through a toiletry bag. Lifting a hairbrush, she squinted into the bristles. The hairs were all blond.

"Ned's," she murmured decidedly.

When she found nothing significant, she headed into the bedroom and opened the closet door. Squinting at the suitcase on the floor, she frowned. She could have sworn Ned had brought two. She would have pondered that longer, but she suddenly crinkled her nose, registering the scent wafting from his clothes. "I'd know it anywhere," she whispered, inhaling the masculine musk she associated with her dream lover.

But no. It had to be her imagination. An odd sensation swept over her, and memory teased her consciousness as if something important was eluding her, staying just out of her reach. Letting her thoughts roam, she found herself replaying her visit with Ned to Castle O'Lannaise—how swiftly Ned had given chase and how surprisingly detailed his description was of the intruder.

Was it possible the man he'd nearly caught had been her lover? After all, Ned's description was a match. And did he know the man? It was possible, since she'd followed her lover here. Had Ned, for some reason, recognized the man and let him go that evening?

She wished she could ask Ned. And she would. But not before she'd searched this place thoroughly. She rifled through the hangers, taking in Ned's loud, button-down shirts, disappointment twisting inside her. What had she expected? To find sand-caked earth sandals and worn jeans?

Her mind raced to the previous night. With her heart thudding against her rib cage, she'd watched in breathless stupefaction as her lover let himself into Casa Eldora as calmly as you please, using a key. Given the way he swept inside, he could have owned the place.

Keeping him in sight, she'd crept from behind the dunes and moved at a crouching run toward Ned Nelson's rental car, which was parked in the driveway.

Ducking behind it, she'd stared at the shingled, stilted house, feeling stymied.

Her first impulse was to rush inside and warn Ned, but the man who'd just left her bed possessed a key to Ned's house, and his manner hadn't been suspicious, which meant Ned probably knew him.

What was the connection? she had wondered, feeling stunned. And more important, did each know the other had a relationship with her? She'd reflected. Her dark, mysterious lover...well, Pansy would believe anything about him, but Ned was a paragon of virtue.

"No," she'd whispered.

Nothing in Ned's behavior had indicated he was privy to the affair. So why was the man letting himself into Ned's house? The more she thought about it, the less sense it made that he was a friend. Ned knew he was free, under the rental agreement, to invite whatever guests he wished. Besides, Pansy had been in Ned's cottage countless times, and she'd seen no sign of a visitor.

She headed for the chest of drawers. What if her lover was an intruder in Ned's home? Should she call the police? She felt torn. She couldn't imagine why he'd enter Ned's home uninvited.

"But he did," she reminded herself.

And after he'd entered the cottage last night, she'd seen nothing more. Venetian blinds in the bedroom had dropped before the light snapped on. After that, she saw only moving shadows.

"What a night," she muttered.

Deciding that donning jeans would take too long, Pansy had risen after her lover left, quickly reached into the closet and grabbed a dress. She was nearly to

Casa Eldora, driving without her headlights, when she'd realized the dress wasn't the wraparound she'd thought, but rather a robe, and that she'd put it on inside out. Fortunately, it was four in the morning, and no one was outside.

Emotions buffeted her—dismay, confusion, worry—but she pushed them all aside as she rifled through Ned's underwear drawer, noting that Ned wore boxer shorts, unlike her lover, who wore briefs. She had no idea what she should feel right now. How could she, before she understood what was going on?

She opened a second drawer without closing the first, then slid her hand beneath a stack of khakis. Her breath caught. She'd found something. "Oh, no," she whispered.

It was a gun! She didn't know much about guns, but she recognized it as an automatic. It was sheathed in a black holster, and when she groped around it, she found a billfold, which she withdrew. Flipping open the leather, she found the last thing she expected—not money, but a blue-and-gold shield. *A New York Police Department badge*, she thought in astonishment. Her eyes trailed over the name engraved on it. Rex Steele. "Who is Rex Steele?" she muttered.

A low, throaty male voice, seemingly coming from nowhere, sounded behind her, startling her. "Me."

Pansy tried to turn, but she was frozen to the spot, one hand gripping the badge, the other the gun. How did he get in here? She hadn't heard him! How long had he been watching her?

The voice came again, sounding silken, almost seductive. "I think you have something that belongs to me."

Her heart thudded hard. The man sounded exactly like her lover! Was he a cop? Her mind raced. Was he working with Judith Hunt? Maybe as an undercover agent on the case involving the *Destiny?*

Or was he lying? Did the badge really belong to someone else? Silently slipping the gun from its holster, she gripped the handpiece, then quickly whirled. Gasping, she realized in shock that it wasn't her lover, after all. She was aiming a gun straight at Ned Nelson's heart.

PANSY LOOKED guilty as sin. As well she should, since she'd broken into his cottage. She looked gorgeous, too, Rex admitted, his eyes noting how the suntan on her cheeks had turned dusky with a crimson blush. Lavender suited her even if the classy, sleeveless, calf-length dress she wore seemed out of keeping with the nine millimeter automatic she was holding in front of it.

She was the last person he wanted to see. In fact, after she'd agreed to marry him, he'd decided never to see her again. He should have known the lady wouldn't make it that simple. He sighed. For years, Rex had been given to understand that his bedroom prowess exceeded normal expectations, but what he wanted was a woman who understood his poetic soul and everyday passions, which was why, awhile back, when he'd jokingly told Truman he might have found a wife, Rex was thinking of the time he'd spent with Pansy as Ned Nelson. Last night, Pansy had made another choice, however, and even though the proposal had left Rex's lips, he was furious.

His eyes settled for a long moment on the perfect

ovals of the manicured, pearl-painted fingernails that were wrapped around the handgrip. Fortunately for him, she didn't realize the safety was turned off. Nor that her slender fingers—so ready to pull a trigger and kill him—had been engaged in loving him less than twenty-four hours ago.

He set his jaw grimly, as if that might ward off the pang at his groin. He tried not to remember just how those hands had looked—threading in his chest hair, gliding over his hips, curling around a mind-stopping erection and caressing it until his thoughts scattered to the four winds. Unwanted heat moved inside him, and vaguely, he was aware he was gauging the number of steps between her, him and the bed.

Not that he'd take her there. As far as he was concerned, their bedroom games were over. If his heart kept hammering when he looked at her...if his breath got shallow and his chest ached...

So be it. Rex Steele had gotten over women before.

He leaned on the doorjamb and stared into the room, trying his best to look casual, thrusting his hands deep into the pockets of the khakis he wore with a bright chartreuse shirt. He fought the urge to remove the uncomfortable, black-framed glasses that were pinching his nose and sent her a long look. "Would you mind lowering the gun?"

Predictably, she went on the defensive. "What are you doing here?" she demanded.

Other than not caring for your tone? "I'm staying here."

"I know that," she huffed, her green eyes steady on his. "I rented the cottage to you, so don't pretend not to know what I mean."

He fought not to react. Without catching Pansy pawing through his things, his mood had been sour enough. Outside, the air was thick and moist with the coming downpour, and if the weather services were right, the storm might be severe. That meant any remaining evidence connected to his father's disappearance would be washed away.

Even worse, at night, before going to Pansy's, he'd been standing watch at Castle O'Lannaise, and while he hadn't yet found anyone lurking around the premises, he was sure someone was there. Which was why he'd come back to the cottage to pick up his gun and badge.

He'd also hired a local guy named Dan McKnight to help keep an eye on the estate, and after picking the front gate's lock for him, Rex had given the man a cell phone. The crusty, retired fisherman was peg-legged and pushing seventy, and when Rex met him, he'd been standing on Sand Road with a sign around his neck. "Jack of All Trades. Will Work." In other words, Dan McKnight was a questionable backup, in Rex's opinion. Not exactly a SWAT team or the Secret Service.

And then there was his proposal to Pansy.

Sighing again, Rex continued staring at her, barely able to believe he'd offered marriage to this woman last night. She'd gotten him so aroused that, in the heat of passion, he'd completely forgotten their circumstances. The truth was, she didn't know anything about him. At least not about the him who showed up nightly, got naked with her and left by dawn.

She'd agreed to marry him, though. Maybe it wasn't fair, but his anger was like the slow burn of aged whiskey to his gut. Marry him on the basis of what? he wondered, his eyes slowly drifting over her. Cash? So she could buy her precious castle? Or good sex?

Great sex, Rex forced himself to acknowledge, blowing out a long, perturbed stream of breath. Torturing himself, he imagined lifting the hem of her lavender dress and listening to it whisper between his fingertips as he whisked it over her head. He knew exactly how her breasts would look—full and heavy, the texture and color of cream. Ripe, they'd start to swell and blush for his hands.

His breath quickened as he thought of the inward dip of her waist and how her tummy might quiver as his ravenous gaze traveled down, settling on the tiny panties she favored, which barely covered the tufts of her honey bush. Dry heat hit the back of Rex's throat, then slid into his limbs. He cursed silently. He was getting hard, and he hadn't even touched her.

At least she was lowering the gun.

As his gaze traced the downward swing of a delicate arm, he was remembering looping kisses along the tender underside. He'd planted the last of them in a sensitive hollow, then bent her elbow to seal the kiss inside. When he finally spoke, his voice was husky, dry and harsh with an edginess he hoped she wouldn't recognize as pure sexual need. He said, "Decide not to shoot me?"

Her eyes stayed locked on his. "I'm still considering."

So was he. Had she really said she'd marry a near stranger just so he'd buy her Castle O'Lannaise? Gold diggers, he thought in disgust, not really believing it, but also not forgetting a conversation he'd overheard between her sisters on the night of the cookout. Apparently Vi and Lily had thought their dates were the lottery winners. Was Pansy, like her sisters, merely trying to land a rich man?

She pushed the gun onto the bureau, gauging its position with her eyes, as if intending to keep it within easy reach. "Who are you?"

"Rex Steele. I thought you figured that out."

"The badge says you're a police officer."

His eyes trailed over the mess of his room—the open drawers and closet. Dryly, he said, "Looks like you're the detective."

She was scrutinizing him suspiciously, looking none too happy when she realized Rex was blocking the only exit. "Are you working for Judith Hunt?"

That took him by surprise, since it was just the opposite. If Judith knew he was here, he'd be incarcerated. He hesitated. "I'm on my own. I work undercover."

"Rex Steele," she repeated.

"I guess," he couldn't help but say. "That is, if you're inclined to believe everything you read."

She blew out a short, peeved breath. "Are you him or not?"

"Yeah."

Her eyes narrowed until they were green slits. "Are you sure?"

"Of course I'm sure." He considered taking off the wig, the glasses, the cheekpads and contacts. Right about now, he'd love to really give her a shock. Besides, the getup was uncomfortable in this heat. When it came to uncomfortableness, even the New York subways in the dog days of August couldn't compete with Seduction Island.

Seduction Island. He contemplated the name. He'd been seduced, all right. "My real name's Rex Steele," he said more convincingly, deciding it was in his best interest to tell the partial truth. "My father was on the *Destiny* when it blew up."

Her jaw slackened, and her eyes hardened. "He's a criminal?"

"You're looking at me as if I've involved sweet, innocent little you in something naughty." Rex couldn't help the words, still not caring for her tone.

"Haven't you?" she asked primly.

More than she knew. For an instant, her hot, panting breath was in his ear, her mouth forming the single word, *More.* "You broke in here," he reminded her. "Not the other way around."

"Are you going to prosecute me?"

Right now, he'd like nothing more, but he couldn't call Judith's attention to him and Pansy. "No."

She stared a long moment. "Well," she suddenly snapped. "Are you going to tell me what's going on?" She sucked in a sudden, sharp breath, her lips parting in surprise. "So, that's why you got to know me. You wanted to find out what I saw the night the boat exploded. That explains all your questions."

It wasn't strictly true, but he didn't divest her of the notion. "My father works for administration at Police Plaza—"

"So, you are from Manhattan," she cut in, her accusatory tone taking him aback.

"I'm trying to give you the information you want," he said levelly. "But you're interrupting me."

The guilty flush rose on her cheeks once more, and

from where he was, her emotional upheaval was palpable. His eyes settled on where the pulse was ticking rapidly at her throat. "Sorry," she muttered. "Go on. Your father's from Manhattan."

"Me, too," he said, pulling his gaze to her eyes. "I think he was pursuing a case on his own and got mixed up with some guys who came here on the *Destiny*. The boat checked out of a slip at the Manhattan Yacht Club on Wall Street."

She offered a grunt of frustration. "What kind of guys?"

"I don't know. That's what I'm here to find out."

"And the boat exploded?" she prompted.

Smart girl. He didn't want to be, but he was impressed with how quickly she was recovering, given the fact that he'd caught her going through his belongings. "Yeah. I came to the island partially at the bidding of my family. I've been pretending to be a tourist, hoping to find him."

"Your family?" she echoed.

He nodded. "I told you about my brothers, Truman and Sully. They're both cops. Our ma's worried sick."

"Those things were true?"

She didn't sound the least bit convinced, and he definitely wished she'd drop the martyred, injured tone. "What things?"

"All the things you told me about your family."

He tried to ignore his heart when it swelled inside his chest. Last night, Pansy might have said she'd marry her phantom lover, but she must have felt something for Ned when he'd told her about the people he loved most. Still, he hated the fact that his tone softened. "Yes."

"Everything?"

He thought back over the anecdotes he'd shared about growing up in the city with his brothers and about his dreams, goals and ambitions. It was the wrong time to notice that Pansy was gritting her teeth to stop her chin from quivering. He'd hurt her.

He braced himself against his emotions, reminding himself she was—at least in a sense—sworn to another man. Even if that man also happened to be him. "Everything," he repeated.

But did all that personal sharing really matter? "What's your problem?" he found himself asking, looking at her wounded eyes and feeling compelled to release a little anger, if only a tenth of what he felt.

Her eyes, touched by hurt a second before, widened. "My problem?"

As far as he was concerned, she'd shown her true colors last night when she said she'd marry a near stranger in order to get her hands on Castle O'Lannaise. Well, he conceded, maybe not a stranger. On at least one level, he'd come to know every feverish inch of her.

"My problem, as you call it," she said coolly, "is that you lied to me." She paused, appraising him frankly, then added, "Ned."

His lips parted in frank astonishment. "I lied?" Instead of answering, she stepped away from the dresser and slipped a hand inside her shoulder bag, checking the contents. He couldn't help but say dryly, "Have everything? I wouldn't want you to forget your keys."

It was hard to tell, but he suddenly decided that the glassy sheen in her eyes, which he'd taken for anger, might be tears. She sniffed. "I thought you were..."

"Goofy Ned Nelson?" he finished, fighting the urge

to stalk closer, knowing he wouldn't be able to keep his hands off her, not once the soft floral scent of her filled his lungs. "Artist. Poet. A sweet guy, not too dangerous. The kind of guy you might introduce to your mother."

"My mother's dead." She shot the words back.

"Sorry," he muttered, lifting a hand and rifling it through the miserable wig.

She stared at him a long, hard moment. "And you seem to misunderstand me, Mr. Steele. I liked Ned Nelson."

Yeah, he wanted to say. *But you preferred a tall, dark, handsome stranger who took your body to the edge of oblivion.* "Is that so?"

"Yes," she defended. As she came toward him, the low heels of her shoes tapped loudly on the hardwood floor. Pausing a second when she reached him, she glanced away, then stepped across the threshold and regally swept past him.

Dammit, he'd known he'd be powerless against her scent. Impulsively reaching, he caught her wrist. At the contact, her face rearranged itself—the chin lifting, the lips pulling into a line—but she didn't draw back. Lifting her gaze, she stared into his eyes almost as if she pitied him.

"Yes, I liked Ned Nelson," she repeated. "He was kind, accepting and understanding. He seemed genuine."

He was genuine. "You've got no right to be mad," Rex said calmly, though he didn't intend to put the rest of his cards on the table. Only he knew she'd been playing night games with someone she thought was another man. For just that second, it was tempting to confront her, but Rex had already seen her in action, and he didn't want to suffer through any denials.

She'd been willing to marry a stranger who could buy her Castle O'Lannaise, and Rex couldn't trust her. It was just that simple. Chalk it up to too many years of dealing with suspects. They'd taught him one thing—to pay attention to what people do, never what they say.

"We were friends," she said simply.

Exactly. "And that was all," he reminded her, his eyes piercing hers. She hadn't wanted Ned Nelson's kiss. On the porch, she'd rejected him. Now the air seemed charged. Over her shoulder, he was aware of how the turbulent clouds of the darkening sky filled a window. Wind was whistling around the cottage.

Her eyes implored. "I met someone," she murmured.

Yeah. Me. "Met?" He was barely able to tamp down his temper. Met? The truth was, she'd said she'd marry him.

"I followed him here," she continued, each word seeming to catch on a coattail of the first, as if she was compelled to speak and her words were chasing each other to a conclusion. "Late last night," she clarified. "Actually early this morning. He let himself in with a key."

He should have known. She hadn't been ransacking the place out of her concern for Ned Nelson, she'd only been following her fantasy man. "That's impossible," he denied, knowing the lies made him just as bad as she was. "I was here all night, asleep."

"I saw him," she insisted.

He shook his head. "Maybe you mistook the house."

She was like a pit bull with her teeth on a toy. "I rent these houses. I didn't make a mistake."

"It was dark."

"The moon was full," she countered.

"It was late. You must have been sleepy."

She was starting to doubt herself. "I know what you're saying, but..."

"And he's your..." Lover? Rex knew very well what the man was to her, but would she admit it?

"Just someone."

He couldn't read the emotion in her eyes. He sure didn't know his own. Pansy had knotted him up like old unsolved cases that were destined to remain mysteries. "Someone," he repeated. "That sounds a little vague, Pansy."

"I don't understand why you're so mad at me," she said. "I'm telling the truth. And I know I'm in your cottage, but...but strange things are happening around here." She added, "And we were friends..."

"Not close enough that you'd share more of your life with me."

"All right," she burst out, jerking her hand from his. "If that's what you want, Ned—" She cut herself off. "Rex," she corrected, making an effort to calm her tone. "I'll tell you about him."

Truly it would be more than he could bear. "Please don't."

"I'm sorry," she whispered.

The only saving grace, he thought, was that he was so good at his job. The suitcase containing his Ned Nelson gear was tucked in the trunk of the rental car, safe from prying eyes, and Rex was used to effortlessly modulating his voice, just as he could change his gestures. Soon enough, he'd do the thing he most excelled at—vanish without a trace. Because of his undercover work, his phone wasn't even listed in his own name. Nor in Ned's, for that matter.

The phone in his pocket rang. Only then did he realize he'd reached for her wrist again. Dropping it, he wondered if that was the last time he'd touch her silken skin. Aware that she was still watching him, he ignored her and dug in his pocket. He drew out the phone, figuring the caller was one of his brothers. "Yeah?"

"It's Old Man McKnight," said a raspy voice. "I think I've got the cuss. You know, that man you been lookin' fer up here?"

"I'll be right there," Rex said, then switched off the phone.

He strode across the room, lifted his gun and badge from where Pansy had left them, then breezed past her, heading for the door. Somehow, when he heard her voice behind him, he managed not to look back.

"You're leaving?"

"Yeah." He tossed the word over his shoulder. "You can let yourself out. Do me a favor and lock up," he added. "I think you've got the key."

Instead she followed him. He heard a gasp of frustration, then the tapping of her shoes. "Where are you going?"

A thousand lies crowded into his mind, but he told the truth. "To your precious castle."

9

REX STEELE had placed a rickety straight-back chair in the middle of the main room at Castle O'Lannaise, and for the past fifteen minutes, Pansy had watched in horrified fascination as he'd questioned the man seated in it. Morphing from sweet Ned Nelson into a seasoned law official, the man with whom Pansy had been spending her evenings expertly befriended his quarry, only to turn around and expose inconsistencies whenever information was repeated.

Rain was falling, but lightly enough that the drops splattering Pansy's dress were nearly dry. Rex had worn a yellow slicker in from the car, and he shrugged out of it in deference to the heat and tossed it onto the window seat. "You worked here then?"

"He's not lying," Pansy ventured, nodding at the tall, rail-thin, dark-haired man. "He's telling you the truth, but you're confusing him. That's Pierre Ludvaux. He used to be the caretaker here."

"She's right about that, she is," seconded Dan McKnight, whom Pansy recognized from years ago, when he worked on the North Shore pier where her daddy used to take her fishing. Obviously a man accustomed to taking his time, Dan glanced through the window, took in the gray sky and rain, which was falling steadily, then turned his attention to Rex. "You see, Mr. Steele, whoever owns this old haunted house decided to save a few buckaroos and let Pierre go."

As Dan hooked his thumbs around the straps of muddy coveralls and maneuvered his peg leg so as not to disturb the candle stubs left by intruders, Pansy noted a cardboard sign propped against the wall that read Jack of All Trades, Will Work, and wondered to which man it belonged.

"That's right," vouched Pierre, the quiver in his voice less discernible now that he had support. "I'm descended from people who came from the mainland to help build Castle O'Lannaise."

Rex eyed him dubiously. "Which is why, generations later, you have such a stake in the place?"

"That's right," defended Pierre. "My family always cared about tradition. Look," he added, "I said I'd tell you anything I can. I'm more than glad to talk to you."

Rex's demeanor said, *Then start talking.* "And so you tend the place free of charge?"

"It's very nice of you," Pansy assured Pierre quickly. "I've cleaned inside the house myself." Hazarding a glance at Rex and still hating his deception even if she was beginning to admit the necessity of it, given what he'd told her about Judith Hunt, she glanced through the window, thinking of times she'd noted small improvements around the estate. "I've sometimes wondered if someone was trimming and weeding."

Rex stared at her, his eyes widening behind his glasses as if she'd intentionally withheld important clues just to torment him, and while she hated being the object of his anger, she also didn't blame him. The man's father had disappeared. Maybe Augustus Steele was dead.

Rex's gaze was pinned on hers, and as she returned his stare, she felt unsettled. It was illogical, but she felt there were eyes lurking behind his eyes, somehow. It was if she was as transparent at Jacques O'Lannaise's ghost, and he could see right through her. Power and intelligence emanated from the man. How could she have missed it before? *Because he's an undercover cop*, she thought, answering herself. And he was apparently good at what he did, too.

No, scratch that. He was excellent. Sensitive, too, she thought, wonder filling her. She forced herself to hold his gaze as she contemplated his drawings and the meals he'd cooked. Sucking in a surreptitious breath, she couldn't help but wonder how he'd look with his shaggy blond locks cut shorter and maybe some wire-rim glasses, then she shook her head, rejecting the notions. No, she loved this man exactly as he was.

Loved. As the word echoed in her mind, she admitted the truth of it. Not that it mattered. Clearly, as far as he was concerned, their friendship was over. Her heart wrenching, she recalled the hurt in Rex's eyes when she'd said there'd been someone else this summer. For an instant, she forgot about Dan and Pierre. She wanted to deny the affair and tell Rex it was over, but wouldn't that be a lie?

Could she end it? Despite her feelings for Rex, she was sometimes sure she couldn't live without the touch of her lover's hands. Shuddering, she recalled the backs of his strong splayed fingers trailing from her waist upward, the nails eliciting a shiver as he prepared to teach her things about her own body she'd never known.

She snapped to attention. "What?"

"You didn't mention that the other day," Rex repeated. "You didn't say you'd suspected someone was tending the grounds."

She couldn't help but react to his tone. "I didn't know I was being interrogated."

He shot her a long, level look. "You are now."

Her lips parted in unspoken protest. She didn't want to explain the lapse, especially not when Rex was sending her a gaze touched with contempt. "I don't know why I didn't mention it, but I..."

"Because she thought the ghost was fixin' the place up, she did," suggested Dan McKnight knowingly. "Isn't that right, miss?"

Damning the older man for being so perceptive, Pansy defensively said, "Of course not. Not really. But..."

"Ya hear so many rumors," encouraged the salty sailor.

"Not just rumors," agreed Pierre. "There're sightings every summer. And storms like the one that's coming are due to Jacques's curse. Everybody knows it."

Rex's audible sigh of perturbed disbelief stopped everyone from continuing. "You say you were doing the landscaping?" he asked, directing the discussion.

He'd emphasized the word *say* as if to indicate Pierre was probably lying. "Yes, but not that anyone noticed. Well, one person can't keep up a place like this, you know." Pierre sucked in a righteously offended breath, and when it hollowed the cheeks of his already gaunt face, Pansy could easily imagine mistaking him for Jacques O'Lannaise, if only on a very, very dark night. "I hate to see the place go to ruin," the man said. "The grass is knee-high, and mice and squirrels are always scuttling down the chimney. My landscaping business is thriving," Pierre added with pride, looking once more as though he might wither under Rex's penetrating stare. "Castle O'Lannaise wasn't my only contract, you know."

"No. But now it's your charity?"

"It's a nice thing for him to do," Pansy said, not wanting to rile Rex but feeling generous toward anyone who shared her love of the estate.

"I don't have to do this work," Pierre added stiffly. "And I might quit," he continued, his tone injured. "All I got for my trouble last week was you trying to tackle me like an NFL linebacker. I was weeding around the hedges when I heard you. Sorry I ran, but you scared me. My night vision's not so hot and, well..."

"The place is haunted," finished Dan graciously. "Always has been, always will be. Nothing to be embarrassed about, Pierre. Bigger men than you have hightailed out of here as if the hounds of hell were on their heels." Dan paused dramatically. "And maybe they were. Yes, sirree, maybe they were."

"I do try to keep the place up," Pierre reiterated.

"Appeases old Jacques's ghost, I bet," said Dan approvingly.

"You never know when the owners might change their minds and decide to fix it up," continued Pierre. "A resort like this could make a lot of money."

Aching, Pansy glanced away. The last thing she

wanted was reminders of the laughter she'd shared in this room with Ned, but with Pierre's words, it came back again. As if the walls still echoed the sound, she could hear her bubbling giggles mixing with his throaty chuckles. Despite the terse tone Ned was taking with her now, she had to believe he'd shared her excitement when they'd spoken of refurbishing Castle O'Lannaise.

She hadn't acknowledged it then, but she swallowed around a lump forming in her throat. Hadn't she found a soul mate? She really was in love with Rex, wasn't she? Not so much because he was a cop, here for the noble purpose of finding his father, but because of what they'd shared—the meals, the dances, the talk. On the porch, when she'd suspected he might withdraw his friendship, she'd started to recognize her feelings. Now that he was clearly going to end their relationship, she felt the pain of loss. As well she should. Wasn't the love of the mind more lasting than the love of the body?

Maybe, her mind answered. But the body couldn't be denied. She sighed, her mind returning to her dream lover. Had Rex been right? Was she mistaken about seeing him at Casa Eldora? It was dark and late, just as Rex had said, and when matters involved her pirate ghost, this wouldn't be the first time she'd been carried away by imagination.

Confusion tore at her as she watched the man she'd started thinking of as her best friend circle the caretaker. Just as she became aware of the wind's low whistle, thunder cracked, and the rain pounded harder, shaking leaf-laden trees and slashing the windowpanes. Feeling edgy, she said, "If you want to continue questioning him, shouldn't we go some-where else?" If the ill-tended sand road washed out, they'd be stuck.

Emotion warred in Rex's features as he glanced to-ward the window. The weather was quickly worsen-ing. He desperately wanted information about his fa-ther, but when his eyes settled on her once more, Pansy could swear he was worried about endangering her. Or was that only wishful thinking? Had he given up on her?

"You're right, Pansy," he said simply, striding to the window seat and lifting the slicker. "Thanks for your help," he said to Pierre. "Sorry I was so tough. I'm just worried about my pop. We'd all better get out of here. The road could wash out."

Pierre didn't move. "Wait," he said suddenly. "Maybe I can help you." The man looked crafty, as if, until now, he'd merely been biding his time, forming an opinion of Rex.

Pansy leaned forward, hoping the information was positive, for Rex's sake, but knowing this would bring an end to whatever she'd shared with the man. Once he got what he wanted, Rex Steele would leave Seduc-tion Island, wouldn't he?

At the thought, her heart squeezed. What was she supposed to do? Marry her nameless lover? In the heat of the moment, it had seemed plausible, but now...

She realized she'd missed the first part of what Pierre had said. "Caught 'im sleepin' in one of the rooms."

"Caught who?" Pansy asked.

Pierre ignored her, his eyes on Rex. "Mind if I see your badge again?"

Rex considered, clearly wondering where Pierre was headed with this, then he reached into his back pocket for the badge. "Sure."

After carefully scrutinizing it, Pierre glanced between Rex, Dan and Pansy. "I swore I wouldn't say anything," he began, lifting a hand and thoughtfully rubbing his chin, "but after Dan caught me here and called you, we got to talking." Pierre added, "Me and Dan go way back. We've known each other for years, though not well. Anyway, he told me you were on the island, looking for your daddy, and that you're not working with the regular cops. Is that right?"

Watchful, Rex nodded. "Yeah. That's right."

Pierre handed back the badge. Sighing, he said, "I hate to break a promise, but I figure you'll know what to do with the information."

"You'd need to give it to me first," Rex murmured.

"Well," drawled Pierre, knowing he had the upper hand now, maybe giving Rex some payback for so mercilessly questioning him. "I found a man here. Sleeping in one of the old feather beds upstairs. He was weak, half drowned and sick with fever. Probably even worse for wear, I figure, given the mites that have set up residence in those feather mattresses."

Pansy's heart skipped a beat, and her eyes shifted to Rex. He hadn't wanted her company, but she'd forced her way into the passenger seat of his car, and during the ride to the estate, he'd explained that he suspected his father was alive. At least he hoped, along with the rest of his family.

"Did he give you his name?" Rex asked.

"I found the fellow a few days after the *Destiny* blew up," Pierre continued, as if he hadn't heard Rex. "He had a burn on his arm—" Lifting a forefinger, Pierre drew a line from elbow to wrist. "Pretty bad burn, too. I would have hauled him down to the hospital, but he was too heavy to lift, so I tried to wake him, using smelling salts from a first-aid kit I keep in the landscaping truck. You know," he added, "in case any of my employees get cut while they're workin'."

When he paused for a breath, Rex softly said, "Go on."

"Not much more to tell, really. He was delirious for the first few days, but he kept mumbling, telling me not to call an ambulance or the police." Pierre shrugged. "I figured he was on the run, that maybe he'd committed some crime, but then..."

"Then?" prompted Pansy.

"Well, as I was nursing him back to health and tending to the burn, he stayed delirious. You know, talking in broken sentences, sleeping most of the day." Pausing, he shook his head. "The evening you two were here...well, he was up and at 'em by then. He had to have seen you. I don't know why he didn't come out and talk. I guess he hid in the attic, but that doesn't make much sense. If you're really his son, he would have recognized you..."

"I don't know," Rex said noncommittally.

Sighing, Pierre looked uncertain. "He said he didn't want the police involved."

When Pansy's eyes slid to Rex, she could see the qualities in him that made her care for him—honesty, integrity and sensitivity. She could also see Rex trying to hide those qualities. No doubt because they wouldn't serve him well on city streets, where he'd have to be tough to protect himself. Around her, he could indulge those qualities, though. Did he know that? She wanted to tell him, but now wasn't the time. Her heart swelled, hurting. Was there something she could do to make him give her another chance?

Reaching into his back pocket, he withdrew a photo of his father and slowly turned it around. "Was this the man?"

Pierre hesitated.

"I'm here to help him," Rex assured.

Pierre nodded slowly. "That's him. Once he got better, he didn't talk much, but when I first found him, he was talking gibberish. From what I could make out, he was a New York cop, married with three kids." Pierre paused. "That's how I recognized your name.

Rex raised an eyebrow. "My name?"

"'Rexie,' he kept saying over and over. He kept saying, 'Rexie, I'm sorry I was so hard on you. I should have helped you go your own way in the world, son. You never wanted to be a cop.' That's what he kept saying," finished Pierre. "That his being hard on you was his one regret. I guess he thought he was dying."

"But he wasn't," murmured Rex, registering his father's deathbed confession.

"No," said Pierre, glancing toward the window. "Which is why I'd have thought your daddy would have gladly taken the opportunity to see you. He wanted to patch things up, I think. Anyway, he's definitely alive."

Just as he finished speaking, thunder clapped so loudly that the walls seemed to shake. For an instant, Pansy thought the windows were exploding inward from a blast. Time vanished, and she was wrenched from a sound sleep by the explosion aboard the *Destiny*. Fire spat into the night, burning until the sea swallowed the wreckage.

But that was over now. The namesake of the vessel on which Jacques and Iris met was destroyed, but Augustus Steele had lived. Just as Pansy fully registered it, the heavens opened, and the deluge began in earnest.

WIND LIFTED the slicker's hem, making the yellow plastic flap wildly. Keeping a hand firmly planted on the hood to hold it in place, Rex ran for the car, biting back a curse as he glided a hand beneath Pansy's elbow to guide her around puddles. Even in this rain, the touch was as electrical as the white, jagged bolts in the sky. Dammit, why had she insisted on coming with him? Her proximity filled him with dark sensual cravings, and he no longer had Dan for a buffer, since the older man had gone in Pierre's truck.

"No offense," Dan had explained without apology, "but a truck's got a better chance on wet sand. Those compacts don't get good traction."

Pushing aside visions of being stuck here alone with Pansy, Rex kept his head low and speeded his steps. *If Ma saw me running through the rain without offering Pansy this coat, she'd kill me*, he thought. Especially since Pansy wore only a silk sheath. But Rex had no choice. In this weather, the wig would fly off, and he wanted to leave Seduction Island without offering explanations.

"I can't believe this wind!"

She'd raised her voice so he could hear her over the

driving rain, and he wished she hadn't. It only reminded him that her voice was made for whispers, just as the jostling of her full, ripe body made him recall—and crave—gentler contact.

"We've got to get out of here," she yelled, raindrops catching on her lips in a way that made him want to kiss them off. "I know we've been expecting it, but I've never seen a storm come up this quick."

It was worsening, too. It was still hot, but the temperature had dropped noticeably. Rex didn't bother to circle the car and open her door. She was already drenched. He got in, reached and unlocked her door from the inside, then slammed his own and turned on the engine. The radio blared, and the windows started to fog as the weather forecaster's voice filled the interior. "A storm warning's been issued for all along the New York coast..."

Quickly shrugging out of the slicker, Rex watched Pansy pass the windshield, her darting figure shadowy, almost ghostly on the other side of the glass. He swiped a spot with his hand so he could see to drive. She lunged inside, bringing a gray sheet of rain through the wedge of the door.

"I can't believe this," she said again, gasping.

As she pulled the door shut against the wind, Rex looked at her and wished he hadn't. His breath caught; his loins tightened. She was drenched to the bone. Her cheeks were wet and ruddy. Her honeyed hair, soaked and darkened by rain, fell onto her bare arms in curling licks. And the dress...

His mouth turned cottony. The dress clung to her, the soaked lavender silk leaving nothing to the imagination. Unbidden, his eyes trailed over her—the rougher texture of a wet lace bra that didn't hide hard, aroused nipples, the inward tuft that marked her navel, the high leg lines of panties he had a sudden urge to peel down her bare, mud-splashed calves.

Somehow, he broke the gaze. "Here," he said, reaching into the back seat and lifting a beach towel. "Use this."

"Thanks." She began toweling her hair. "Sorry about the car...the seat..."

Doing his best to ignore the urge to rip off the wig, tell her who he was and make love to her in the front seat of the car, he put the vehicle into gear and pulled out, trying to concentrate on the weather report. "At North Point Shore," said the man's nondescript voice, "winds are gusting at fifty miles per hour. Discussion has begun about whether residents of Seduction Island should evacuate..."

Hunching over the wheel, he peered into the darkness, switching on the high beams to penetrate the rain, figuring it didn't matter since few people would be foolish enough to get caught in this. Suddenly, he was conscious of her again. She sighed deeply, as if in relief, and once more he felt himself getting hard. That sigh, he thought. It was exactly how she sighed after she came.

"Thank God we're going to make it off the hill," she said, sounding breathless. "I'm so glad your father's alive."

He nodded. "Me, too." His voice was low, his mind filling with thoughts of the woman beside him even as his heart flooded for his father. His father's voice ghosted in his mind, not Pierre's, when the words replayed. *I should have helped you go your own way in the world, son. You never wanted to be a cop.*

Augustus had thought he was dying, and yet his last words were for Rex. Maybe that's what Rex had been waiting for all these years, just some acknowledgment from the old man that Rex hadn't turned out like his other sons. Yes, it must have been, because Rex felt better, freer to pursue his own life. Funny, he thought, glancing at Pansy, just when he thought he'd found his life, he'd lost it again.

"Do you think you'll find him?"

He shook his head, simultaneously wondering what was going through her mind about the rift between them and trying to tell himself he didn't care. "From what Pierre said, Pop disguised himself and left town. My guess is he's in Manhattan."

"The day we spent at the estate, he must have seen us," she said, offering him an unwanted reminder of how he'd felt that day, so happy to have found a woman with whom he could share his dreams and visions. "Why didn't he come out of hiding and talk to you?"

Because I was in disguise. Just weeks before, his mother hadn't recognized him. No doubt his father hadn't, either. "Your guess is as good as mine."

Her voice hitched with emotion. "Not because he didn't want to talk to you, I'm sure. It was powerful," she murmured, "what Pierre overheard your father saying about you...about your relationship. Don't you two get along? You told me so much about your mother and brothers..."

But not Pop. "We get along." He leaned closer to the windshield and concentrated on the storm, not wanting to open himself to her now. "We're just not as close as we'd like."

"You didn't want to be a cop?"

Previously, he'd liked her inquisitiveness. Now Rex wanted to drop her off and leave town. He shook his head. "Not really."

"What did you want to be?"

Married to a woman who talks with me the way you do— and whose lovemaking keeps me up until dawn. He shrugged. "Poet. Painter. Chef."

Her voice was tentative. "You could do any of those things in a town such as this. Work odd jobs to make ends meet. People do it all the time."

He shot her a long look. "Are you really suggesting I move here, Pansy?" *Why not just lay it on the line?* His voice lowered yet another notch and turned husky, impassioned by his conflicted emotions. "What? So you can carry on the relationship you've been enjoying with Ned Nelson? Maybe you'll ask me to accompany you to Castle O'Lannaise so you can look for your fantasy pirate?" Or, as he knew, for the man with whom she'd been sharing nights of explosive pleasure.

"I wasn't suggesting anything," she said stiffly. "But I want you to be happy. If the security of being an officer held you back from pursuing dreams—" She rested a hand on his arm. It felt so warm and soft he seriously considered pulling over, hauling her against him and kissing her.

"You're already all those things you want to be," she said. "Poet. Painter. Chef. If you're willing to struggle a little, you can live that life."

Pansy didn't know it, but he wouldn't even have to

pinch pennies. If he wanted, he could buy her castle. Maybe he'd have done it, he thought, if she'd come clean with him. Instead, she was acting as if she wanted more from him while in reality she'd accepted a marriage proposal.

"What stopped you from living that life?"

Wanting his father's love so badly. And now he wanted hers. Was he a man destined not to find any love at all? Before he could answer her question, the cell phone rang. Taking a hand from the wheel, he retrieved it from his pocket. "Maybe Pierre's stuck," he guessed.

Sighing as if she'd prefer to continue their discussion, she said, "I hope not."

Flicking on the phone, Rex tucked it under his jaw. "Yeah?"

"It's Sully. I got the word that Judith pulled her guys out of the water. Sounds like there's a bad storm brewing where you are. Is that rain I'm hearing?"

"It's coming down hard," he returned. "Lightning, thunder, the works. Anyway, we need to talk. I was just about to call you—"

"It's better that I found you. All hell's breaking loose in the city. Ma's starting to believe Pop's dead. She was asking me if I think we should start making arrangements. And Judith may be on the island, but she's also keeping daily contact with the head brass at Police Plaza—"

"If you'll let me talk," Rex began, the soft scent of Pansy's rain-washed skin pulling into his lungs as he spoke.

Ignoring him, Sully continued. "Truman and Trudy are trying to find out what Judith knows about Pop.

She definitely wants to do him damage. Dimi Slovinsky, that's Trudy's boss over at the *News*, says he'll keep an ear to the ground for us, just in case there was some previous altercation between Judith and Pop that we don't know about. Trudy says—"

"I found Pop."

A pause followed, then a surprised-sounding voice said, "Huh? Why didn't you tell me? What's going on?"

It wasn't like Sullivan Steele to talk before hearing the facts. Deliberation was more his style—except when it came to Judith, with whom he'd long been going head-to-head. "Pop's been holed up on an old estate here named Castle O'Lannaise," Rex reported, then he filled his brother in on the details.

After he was finished, Sully said, "Sounds like you've done all you can."

Feeling Pansy's eyes studying him, Rex forced himself to finish the conversation. "I'll be out of here tomorrow, big brother. I'll catch the first ferry in the morning. So far, they're not evacuating, and given the storm I'm seeing through this windshield, it's tough to call. Anyway, I'll see you tomorrow. I'm definitely coming home."

HOME.

Pansy was wet to the bone, and the defroster in the compact had activated the air-conditioner, so she was fighting shivers by the time they reached the house built so many years ago by her ancestor Winston Hanley. A power outage had claimed the lights on the South Shore, and static had made listening to the radio impossible.

She stared through the windshield at a wall of rain, barely able to make out her house. Water and wind were shifting the shapes of the dunes, and debris, probably from trash cans on the beach, flew through the air like tumbleweeds. Dark figures were darting on the lawn, and with a start Pansy realized they were her sisters. Fighting nearly gale-force winds, they were shuttering the windows. Pansy's hand closed over the door handle. If it weren't for the storm, she would have bolted from the car. At least that's what she told herself. Maybe she would have run before she and Rex Steele had left Castle O'Lannaise. Her heart ached, but she was tired of his attitude. "Can't we talk this out?"

He knew what she meant. "I don't think so."

"If you'd talk to me," she ventured, hating the pleading tone creeping into her voice. "Just tell me what I did that was so wrong. I know you caught me in your house, but..." Swallowing hard, she tried again. "Just talk to me. Before now, we were so good at talking to each other."

His voice was silken, almost seductive. "I wouldn't worry over much about it, Pansy. After all, it isn't talk that makes a woman like a man, now, is it?"

Her whole body tensed. "I offered to tell you about the other person I was seeing."

"Other person? Is that what we've been doing?" he asked, leaning so close to her in the car's shadowy interior that she could feel his breath teasing her cheek. "Seeing each other?"

"Yes," she said.

"I don't think so," he returned. "If you'd been interested, you would have kissed me that night on your porch."

"Feelings change."

"Why? Because now you know I'm a tough guy?"

She was starting to suspect he'd take anything she said and twist it around. On a rush of anger, she turned to him. "So, this really is it for us, Rex?" she asked, barely able to control her temper. "You're going home? Just like that? You're not even going to make plans to keep in touch?"

He hesitated. Neither his glasses nor the contacts he wore—probably, she supposed, to enhance his already blue eyes—could hide his emotion. Or his desire.

When he didn't answer, she continued. "You're not as cool as you think, Rex Steele." The heat of aroused passion was bringing hot color to her cheeks, and she was glad to finally get this off her chest. "I've seen how you look at me—" Her voice hitched as she said the words, and she felt jittery inside, barely able to believe she was saying it.

"How's that?"

She hated him for pretending not to understand. She recalled his gaze when she'd lunged inside the car, his sharp intake of breath when he realized the fabric of her dress was soaked and transparent. The whole time he was driving, his eyes kept coming back to her body as if drawn by a homing device. "How you look at me?" she murmured, her voice lowering as she suddenly, impulsively reached out and lifted a finger to his face. Simultaneously, he leaned back, catching her finger against his cheek. "Rex," she said simply, "you look at me as if you want to rip off my clothes."

He dropped her finger as if he'd been burned.

"I feel I know you so well," she said. "And yet not at all."

And then she grasped the door handle, pushed open the door and ran toward home, shielding a face that was blinded by the storm.

10

"YOU'RE COMING WITH US, Pansy!" Vi shouted hours later when a horn sounded, its blare muted by the storm. Clad in slickers, Vi and Lily were holding a board over the remaining French door to Pansy's room while Pansy nailed it into place. Suddenly, the howling wind lowered, its whistle spiraling downward as if being sucked through a drain. In the lull, Vi's voice was clear, high-pitched and scared. "That's Lou. He's out front in the Jeep! He's already picked up Garth! C'mon, we've got to go! If you try to leave later in your car, you might not make it! The bridge might wash out."

Bracing her palm against the board, Pansy drew back the hammer and pounded, swinging her head as she moved. The wind caught wet strands of her hair, whipping them from her eyes. The slicker's hood blew back, formed a cup behind her neck and began collecting rain. She sputtered as water splashed into her mouth. "Go on!" she screamed, ignoring the water gushing under her collar. "I can finish shoring up the house!"

Vi yelled, "It's good enough now. This'll hold! Let's go!" Turning, Pansy saw Lily's mouth move. Her voice seemed to follow a second too late as if the wind carried off her words and then brought them back, making them seem oddly out of synch with the motions of her lips. "They're already advising people to take the ferry, not the bridge, in case the bridge washes out."

"We won't let you stay!" Vi insisted. "We can't! Why aren't you coming?"

Because Rex might be on the island. He'd told his brother he was leaving in the morning. Or had he changed his mind? If he'd gone, had he taken the rental car or the ferry?

Pansy gritted her teeth in frustration. They'd lost their parents in a storm, so Pansy understood her sisters' sentiments. Why hadn't she stayed in the car and told Rex how deep her feelings were? If she had, she could leave in good conscience.

But as soon as she'd run inside the house, she'd panicked. On impulse, she'd called Manhattan directory assistance. She'd needed to know where to find Rex if he really broke contact with her, but he hadn't been listed. Probably because he worked undercover. Which meant a precinct wouldn't give out his number. Pansy wouldn't know which precinct to call, anyway. This might be her only chance to talk to him again!

"We've got to go!" shouted Vi.

"One more second!" Bracing herself, Pansy lifted the hammer, reflexively tightening her grip as the wind threatened to wrench it from her hand. Hanging on, she drove a final nail home. *Good*, she thought. *This should hold. I'll be safe.*

At least she hoped so. "Done!" Whirling, she pocketed the hammer, grasped the sleeves of her sisters' slickers and ran toward the front door. Ducking their hooded heads, the women pushed against the wind's current. In the worst gusts, tree trunks arched and limbs bowed toward the ground; weighted by wind and rain, the topmost branches of saplings swept what was left of sand roads; seaweed and debris blew wildly, and the shoreline vanished as water ate its way inland, claiming lifeguard chairs and public trash cans.

Pansy grasped the doorknob and pushed. Wind caught the door, swinging it inward. All three women entered, then pushed from behind to shut it. Leaning against it, they gasped. "Don't worry," said Pansy breathlessly, the silence of the foyer deafening compared to the noise outside. "I'll get the next ferry."

"If the storm gets worse," said Vi, grabbing an overnight bag she'd left near the door, "there may not be another ferry, Pansy, and if the bridge washes out, you'll be stuck."

Lily was grabbing a duffel. "Are you sure Lou and Garth are out there, Vi? I couldn't see in this mess."

"I heard the horn. He's definitely here." Vi whirled on Pansy. "You can't stay!"

But she had to. Pansy couldn't explain it, but she knew she couldn't leave. Maybe because, once again, star-crossed lovers were being separated by a storm. Unlike Iris, Pansy was going to stay and set things right. "Here—" She reached into the drawer of a curio cabinet in the foyer, withdrawing a letter she'd sealed in a Baggie. "When you get on the ferry, look for Rex Steele."

Her sisters stared at her blankly. It took Pansy a moment to realize they'd never heard the name. "Ned," she corrected. "Ned Nelson."

"Who is Rex Steele?" exclaimed Vi. "Right now,

you don't even remember Ned's name! What's going on?"

Lily had shouldered her duffel, and her hand was on the doorknob. She groaned. "I should have known. This has something to do with your obsession with Jacques O'Lannaise, doesn't it? I know it does! It's the only reason you'd act this illogical!"

Vi gasped. "What?"

Lily grabbed Pansy's shoulder. "We lost Mom and Dad this way. Iris died in a storm. We're not going to lose you."

"I'm going to be fine," Pansy assured. "But if Ned's on the ferry, promise me you'll give him this letter."

"I knew it!" exclaimed Lily. "You do think history is repeating itself!"

As Vi leaned and hugged Pansy, she snatched the letter from her hand. "If he's there, of course we'll give it to him. But be careful. You promise, sis? We've got to go!"

"Promise," Pansy whispered, her throat aching with emotion.

Lily kissed her cheek. "Don't wait too long. Another ferry should run in a half hour."

And that one, they knew, really might be the last. "I'll be there," Pansy said. But it was a lie. As soon as they were gone, she was heading to Casa Eldora to look for Ned.

"NED? NED?"

At first he didn't recognize the name or the voice. When he finally turned, Rex was facing Vi. She was dressed in a calf-length yellow slicker exactly like the one he wore and she was also encumbered by an orange life vest she'd been issued upon boarding. With the hood of her slicker up, hiding her shorn hair, Vi looked astonishingly like her sister.

"Ned," Vi repeated, sounding relieved. "Pansy's not here, but she said to give this to you."

For hours, Rex had been telling himself he'd be able to forget Pansy. He couldn't believe the idiocy of these women. Hadn't they noticed there was a storm raging outside? "To give me what? Where is she? Why isn't she here?"

"She said she was staying."

Had Pansy lost her mind? He glanced around, expecting to see her elbowing through the stranded vacationers who filled the boat. Surely, Vi was joking. As the storm picked up, he'd been so intent on packing he hadn't even taken the time to get rid of the bothersome garb he'd been wearing. Which was just as well, since without the disguise, Vi wouldn't have recognized him. "She didn't come with you?"

"I think she's catching the next boat."

If there was one. They were still docked, waiting for the captain's go-ahead. "Maybe she'll make this one."

"I don't think so."

He cursed softly, gazing to sea. Ferries ran on the bay side, but even here, the water was rough. The bow and stern were dipping dangerously low. A mile off, a finger of land led to another larger island the locals referred to as the mainland, mostly for the sake of convenience. The real mainland was another few miles away. "Why isn't she here?"

"I don't know." Vi glanced around, trying, Rex realized, to keep an eye on Garth, who was in the crowd, tightly holding Gargantua's leash. He also spotted

Lily and Lou, not to mention Judith Hunt. The kid he'd noticed at the town meeting was seated on his mother's lap, looking green around the gills. Vi continued. "Lily thinks Pansy's staying has something to do with Castle O'Lannaise—"

"What?" Rex exploded.

"I don't know," said Vi, "but Lily thinks Pansy believes that, somehow, history is repeating itself."

"How?"

Vi shrugged. "I don't know. But, like I said, she wanted you to have this. Here. I've got to catch up with Garth and Lily. Everybody's looking for seats."

Glancing down, Rex braced himself against the sudden missed beat of his heart. It was a letter, sealed in plastic. He'd know the stationery anywhere. It was thick, cream-colored stock, and the writing on the envelope looked like Iris Hanley's. Why would Pansy send him one of Iris's letters? And why would she risk doing so now, in a storm that could destroy an artifact she loved?

Carefully, he drew the letter from the plastic, then from an envelope. He scanned the first lines.

Dearest—

   If you get this, then history has been reversed. You'll be on a boat sailing away, while I remain on this island, searching for you in the storm. We are a bit like Jacques and Iris, aren't we?

Rex lifted his gaze, realizing the letter wasn't one of Iris's, after all. Pansy had used the same stationery— she'd told him it was still manufactured—and her handwriting was nearly identical to Iris's.

A voice came over a loudspeaker. He tilted his head, straining to hear. It was the captain. They were preparing to leave the dock.

His eyes dropped hungrily to the words she'd written.

Earlier, I shouldn't have left you in the car. I should have stayed and fought, so you'd know how I feel. I love you. Now, I'm afraid I'll never see you again.

There was someone else this summer, as you know, and now you can't stop me from telling you about him. We had an affair that was physical, powerful and satisfying—I admit that!—but it's you I want to know. I want you to come back! I won't see him again! The affair's over! How much more powerful it would be to explore that sensuality with a man you love! For me to explore that sensuality with you!

Years ago, my sisters and I promised never to date tourists. We said they'd always leave us, that they'd always break our hearts. Don't break my heart, Rex!

Don't forget me!
You have my love, Pansy

The vessel was groaning in the water, preparing to pull away from the dock, and Rex's blood was racing with desire and panic. He strode toward the exit, hoping there was still time to get off.

REX HADN'T BEEN at Casa Eldora. "Thank God," Pansy whispered, since that meant he'd made the ferry. Yes, he was probably safe on the mainland by now, while she was still searching for him.

"Pull over and think," Pansy muttered, but she knew stopping would be the kiss of death. Even high beams didn't penetrate the rain. The wipers swept water away, leaving patches of murky darkness the instant before another deluge. Debris kept hitting the car, too—ricocheting off the hood, scratching the windows. She was terrified of hydroplaning. Stalling would be worse. She'd be stranded, vulnerable, and she couldn't let that happen.

Her eyes darted to the bleak, dark landscape, looking for help, but if she'd passed any law enforcement or EMS vehicles, she hadn't been able to see them. She was all alone.

She shivered, barely able to make out the road. So many people were gone that the sirens had ceased. Swallowing hard, she tried to think of what she'd do if she stalled. In moments when the wind died, she'd be able to walk, but if it gusted, she'd be swept off her feet.

"What are you doing?" she whispered to herself. What phantoms had she been chasing this summer? She'd never know the identity of her dream lover. She'd accepted that. Even if he came to her again, he'd never reveal himself.

And what kind of love was that? A mirage, she thought. Sinful and satisfying, yes. But still a mirage. She'd never forget him—not his bold hands. Or how he'd kissed her breasts, thrusting his tongue until she thought she'd die from pleasure. Or how he'd looked, naked and hard, his dusky sex aroused and surrounded by silken tangled curls.

"A mirage," she whispered.

She'd lost a real man, Rex Steele, because of a tempting mirage. She'd lost a soul mate because a stranger had brought her body enjoyment beyond her wildest imaginings. Worse, she'd stayed here, hoping to win Rex back, and she'd put herself in serious danger.

She should have listened to her sisters. She should have known Rex would do the sensible thing and leave. Damn her romantic mind for thinking he was like Jacques O'Lannaise, that he'd stay here as she had, determined not to leave until they could do so together.

Yes, tonight she was still chasing phantoms. Like Jacques, she was wandering the island in a storm, searching for love.

But her love was gone.

"Keep driving," she whispered. Maybe she'd make the ferry.

11

"WINDS GUSTING over a hundred..." Rex strained to hear, but static was breaking up the words on the radio. "North Shore bridge closed...no more ferries to the mainland...power outages..."

At least he'd gotten over the bridge. Realizing Rex was going to look for Pansy, Lou Fairchild had offered him the Jeep, something that earned Lou a sloppy, wet kiss from Lily, who'd promptly wreathed her arms around his neck. Given the shocked look on Lou's face, he'd happily have thrown in anything else he owned for just one more such kiss.

Under other circumstances, Rex would have laughed. Vi and Lily had begun relationships believing Garth and Lou had won the lottery, but now the women were obviously involved for other reasons. It was definitely not the time to contemplate other people's relationships, however. Rex needed to concentrate on his own, so he'd grabbed the keys and bolted, barely making it off the ferry before it pulled from the dock.

Peering at the windshield, he felt a renewed rush of gratitude for the Jeep, not to mention the first-aid kit, industrial flashlight and flares he'd found inside. In the compact, he wouldn't have stood a chance. He hoped Pansy hadn't tried to leave. Surely she'd stayed put, knowing her little black car would be swallowed whole by the pitch-black night. At times, the winds touching down were strong enough to lift such a vehicle.

"No," he muttered. "She'd never go outside in this." Rex's hands tightened on the wheel. His jaw was set, his gaze narrow, focused, unblinking. Led by glimmers from the headlights, he used flashes of trees bordering the road to guide him. Twice, he'd almost wrecked. Suddenly, he swerved. He'd almost run off the road! Dammit, he wished he could see better! Power was out all over the island, and windows were boarded, so even if people were still inside houses, candles and lanterns wouldn't serve as beacons. He had to reach Pansy. She'd said she loved him!

"Two rescue vehicles down..." A barely comprehensible voice broke through the static. "Remain inside your homes..."

When static reclaimed the radio, it felt to Rex as though he was the only person left alive in the world. But Pansy was nearby. She had to be!

He couldn't see anything through the brackish water slushing across the darkened windshield. Her house was around here somewhere, though. He was sure of it. Judging by the odometer, he was a mile past a cottage he'd recognized. Which meant the Hanley home should be right here, but he saw absolutely nothing. What if she was in danger? He had to find her!

In a flash of lightning, he suddenly saw the thick trunk of a huge tree coming right toward him. Rushing water had washed away topsoil, exposing gnarled roots. Just before the world went black again, he saw...her.

Wrenching the wheel sharply, he felt the tires lift, hydroplaning on a wave that brought the Jeep broadside. He braced himself for impact, praying the tree wouldn't hit the driver's side. But nothing happened except the engine stalled. The power went out. The lights on the dashboard blinked off. He clicked off the ignition and tried the engine, his mind denying what he had just seen...or thought he'd seen.

It was dark, he reminded himself. Eerie, dangerous. No doubt, his mind was playing tricks. He could have sworn he'd seen Pansy, though, standing in front of the tree, waving him away from it, her figure illuminated by lightning. A heartbeat later, he'd realized it wasn't Pansy. The woman was wearing an old-fashioned long dress and shawl.

He was losing his mind, Rex thought, turning the key again. The Jeep had flooded. He took a deep breath. It was so dark, and the rain was so heavy, that he couldn't make out his hands on the wheel. He could swear he'd seen a woman in front of the tree. Iris? The name of Pansy's ancestor ghosted through his mind.

Yeah, right, he thought, trying to steady his nerves. Was he really thinking that Iris Hanley's ghost had just saved him from wrecking?

No, of course not. It was only an illusion, a weird confluence of glinting headlights and colors from nature producing a mirage. When he'd begun to swerve, he'd imagined her flying away, her body evaporating into a fluid, transparent trail that wove through the trees as if she were made of wind. Wind, he thought, that was headed toward Castle O'Lannaise. It was as if the storm had unleashed Iris's ghost, and she were traveling to meet her lover.

"That's something Pansy would make up," he whispered, pushing the thoughts aside. He felt around in the passenger seat for the flashlight, knowing better than to leave the relative safety of the Jeep. The winds were strong enough to lift a man. Flying debris could kill him. For all he knew, live wires from downed poles were lying in the gushing rivulets. He'd never know how long he waited, sitting in darkness, his hand gripped around the flashlight, listening to the rain pound against metal.

And then, in the jagged white flash of another lightning bolt, he saw the Hanley house. It appeared, then vanished in a poof as if someone had just taken a picture. An image like a negative lingered just long enough for him to register the water eddying around the house. It wasn't rainwater, he realized, feeling the closest thing he'd ever known to terror. It was the ocean, lapping the foundation.

If these were his last moments, he decided, there was only one place he wanted to spend them—in Pansy Hanley's arms. Gripping the flashlight, he pushed open the Jeep's door. As he stepped out, he felt the madly whirling wind catch him from behind and lift him from the ground.

This gives a whole new meaning, Rex thought, *to being swept off your feet.*

REX WAS SAFE. That was the only thought sustaining Pansy. Hours ago, wind had lifted the board nailed over the French doors, wrenching it from the house. Seconds later, debris had smashed the panes inward,

and ever since, wind had been rushing through the
house's interior, howling. If only her sisters hadn't
been in such a rush, Pansy thought, she would have
nailed the board more securely. An old line from
somewhere flitted through her consciousness. If
horses were wishes, then beggars would ride.

Downstairs, something crashed. Curtains rustled.
Rain was hammering a house she couldn't see out of,
since most windows were boarded or shuttered from
the outside. Dressed in jeans and a blouse, Pansy hovered on an upstairs bed, her fisted hands clutching the
duvet as she stared through the only uncovered window.

Nothing could be seen. Just rivulets rushing down
the panes. Oh, no, that was water downstairs, wasn't
it? She started. She kept imagining she heard the
ocean gushing inside, climbing the steps like an in-
verse waterfall. Earlier, during a lull, she'd seen how
close the ocean's waves were.

Soon, the house would float, she imagined. Or wind
would rip it from the foundation and it would fly
across the sky, like Dorothy's house in *The Wizard of
Oz*. Or maybe it wouldn't happen that way at all. No,
maybe a tidal wave would simply surge over her.

She wished she could see Rex again. Just once, she
thought, just his face. She wished she had a picture of
him. And she hoped her letter had reached him. He
had to know how she felt! That he was her summer
lover! As for her dream lover, she was sure he, too,
was gone. She had memories, of course. Visions of her
sultry summer and the searing sex that had freed her
to enjoy herself as never before. *Please bring Rex
back...let me share that with him.*

She wanted—no, needed—to make that kind of love with a man who understood her mind and shared her passions. *But it's too late,* she thought, a sob welling in her throat. Backing up, she wedged herself into the corner created by the wall and headboard, then she drew her knees against her chest. She told herself she wasn't really waiting for the end to come. No, everything would be all right, wouldn't it? The storm would be over soon.

She stared into the room, which was illuminated by a weak, yellow-white lick of candle flame that danced wildly with the wind. The walls were lost to shadows and darkness, but Pansy could see the curtains dance, too. The movements seemed surreal, like something from a Disney cartoon.

For a brief second, she visualized other objects in the room—the chairs, armoire and bookshelves—dancing and singing, and then, delirious with fear, she thought of Rex again. Casa Eldora had been vacant, which meant he'd gotten to the mainland. He was definitely okay. And she was lucky to have made it home.

By the time she'd gone to the root cellar for supplies, the space was flooded with salt water, and the lanterns stored there were wet. She considered upending a flashlight, but she didn't want to waste batteries, and although her clothes were damp from all the exploration, she didn't want to hunt in the dark to try to borrow something of Lily or Vi's.

Suddenly, she gasped and rose to her knees on the mattress. She'd heard her name! But no, she thought with dismay, sinking onto her haunches, that was only wishful thinking. She was probably the sole person left on the island. She felt so alone that her imagination had kicked into high gear. The house was big. The French doors accessible. Anybody could come in...

Even ghosts.

She shuddered. Moments ago, she could have sworn she saw a trailing tail of... She wasn't sure what. Smoke? she wondered. Fog? Whatever it was had circled before the window, then shot off in the direction of Castle O'Lannaise. But that was crazy! Nothing was visible through the window but rain.

"Pansy?"

Her heart clutched. She stared through the doorway into the black recess of the hall, her voice catching, sounding high-pitched and terrified. "Hello! Hello! Is someone here?"

Only the wind answered. She got to her feet, then crouched on the bed, ready to lunge if she needed to. Suddenly, she shrieked. The ghost of Jacques O'Lannaise loomed from the shadows, his broad shoulders filling the doorway, his raven hair slicked back by rain.

A second later, she thought it was her dream lover. Confused, thinking she'd gone over the edge, she watched in shock as he moved toward her, then realized he was dressed in the clothes she'd last seen Rex wearing. His face wasn't sculpted, though, but fleshed out, his cheeks full.

Or were they? She watched in stupefaction as he reached inside his mouth and removed two white pads. Almost magically, his face was transformed into that of her phantom lover. Had those pads always been in his mouth? She was off the bed in a flash, gaping. "It was you!"

He looked at her as if he'd seen a ghost, as if he'd

been sure he'd never see her again. Rain poured from him. Had he really been outside in this? she wondered, awed. She wrenched her head toward the window. No man could have made it to the house from a car. How had Rex Steele done so? "What's going on?" she cried, staggering forward, her hands instinctively grasping his shoulders for support, then pushing off the slicker, which fell to the floor. "It was you!" she repeated.

His kiss was the only answer. Hot and wet, his mouth swooped down and consumed hers. A hand splayed on her chest, glided up her neck and held her chin in place so that his tongue could plunge deep, deeper. Hungrily, she flicked against it, her tongue as fast and hot as the candle flame in the room. It danced in his mouth, the way the wind was making the world dance. Gasping, she felt him through his drenched khakis. He was hard and bursting for her, and she throbbed, wanting all that male heat that yearned to be inside her.

Wet lava spun from her core while her tongue simulated the motions of her hips. His clothes were plastered to him, she thought as she tried to tear them off, her mind hazing at the taste of a mouth she'd thought she'd never kiss again. She didn't know how this had happened. She didn't care. Right now, she had what she wanted, what she thought she'd never have again

This man who understood all of her.

Greedily, his hands—so big and warm and wet— tore at her shirt, ripping down the buttons, pushing fabric toward her shoulders. As she undid his shirt buttons, he single-handedly unhooked her bra. His mouth never left hers, not even for a breath, as if he feared breaking their kiss might end it forever.

Released, her firm, high breasts brushed him, her already hard nipples almost stinging, straining with heat as they swept across the wet fur pelt of hair covering his chest. Moans came from deep in her throat. Smothered by his mouth, the trapped sound seemed otherworldly, as surreal as the storm crashing around them.

They might die, but not even that could explain this urgency. She needed his flesh—warm, living and gushing inside her because she loved him. And he loved her. He must have gotten the letter and returned! His lips were drinking, suckling. He pulled her tongue deep into his mouth with his as their hands grasped and fumbled, desperate to pull down their pants. His were so wet that her hand slipped on the fabric, and he arched, bucking as her hand slid over an erection. Even through his clothes, it burned, throbbing at her touch. And still, his mouth was locked to hers, turning softer and moister, his roving tongue shooting warm, liquid sensations along her veins. She felt as though she'd been ripped open, every nerve exposed for him to touch.

Jagged, edgy need hitched her emotions higher as she felt his hands kneading her breasts. He leaned away just once, as if to watch the aroused, pink tips darken. She raked down his zipper, and as she felt his flesh push through the boxer shorts, she shuddered. Her knees weakened when the silken length was in her hand. Relief flooded her at that glorious touch. She thought she'd never hold him again, never feel this again. She wanted everything with him—to take him into her mouth, lick him, tease him. She wanted to make him beg for what she most wanted to give.

Both her hands found him and stroked. His fingers found her, too. They molded over her, cupping and fondling, then thick fingers pushed inside, leaving her dripping and shaking.

There were no condoms tonight. He had none. Neither of them cared. Still standing, she guided him to her, but he urged her onto the bed. As her bare back hit the mattress, her eyes fell to him, her breath stopping, her throat drying. A soft pant came from between her lips as she fixed her eyes on the most intimate part of him; she studied every detail, stopping when she saw the drop of moisture on the tip. Oh, she wanted him so much she was trembling.

His hands were curling over her knees, gently pushing them, slowly caressing her thighs. As she parted for him, she felt him lift her knees slightly, to better view where she'd opened like the petals of a flower. She nearly climaxed from just the heat of that gaze studying every open inch, her eyes drifting to him once more. She'd never wanted anything so badly in her life.

She couldn't wait. Aching, she whimpered. Her hands grasped his shoulders and pulled him toward her. Joy flooded her when his weight came crushing down on her, and she felt as if she was spiraling downward in a whirlwind. She was so ready, slippery and waiting, and she moved a hand between them, offering encouragement by caressing him.

He reacted with a deep, shaking moan and then, with a sudden swift stroke, he entered her. There was no pausing, no guiding. Just another sound of satisfaction and a deep thrust that opened her legs farther. She felt this was endless, that he'd never stop filling her. Moving, he began loving her with his whole length, every searing inch.

Shuddering, he reached beneath her, the flat of his palms gliding under her buttocks, their rubbing skin feeling as soft as water as he lifted her, angling her hips so he could go deeper still. She arched, wanting him as fully as he could come into her. "It was you," she whispered again, senselessly, her fingers curling over his shoulders, digging into his skin.

It didn't matter, of course. If they made it safely through the storm, they would have a lifetime for explanations. If not, they both wanted it to end like this—riding together through the stormy night, locked in an embrace so tight that even this gale couldn't pass between them.

"Who are you?" She whispered the words. Feeling him tense inside her, spasming and clenching, ready to shoot, she arched upward, climbing high for her climax, her whole body begging for his to come, wanting to share this joy. "Who?"

"Yours," Rex answered hoarsely, jaggedly. Gasping as pleasure claimed him, he kept saying, "Yours. Yours. I'll always be yours, Pansy Hanley."

_____Epilogue_____

CIRCLING HER ARM more tightly around Rex's waist the next morning, Pansy bit back a smile as Judith Hunt put her hands on her hips, exhaled a dissatisfied breath and surveyed the wreckage. Her dark blue eyes took in every detail, her crimson-painted lips curling downward as if yesterday's storm had touched down on earth for no other reason than to spite her. Despite the circumstances, her long dark hair was perfectly combed, and she was tastefully dressed in a soft gray suit. Sand dusted the tops of practical gray flats.

Pansy and Rex, having just arisen from bed, had decided to walk along the beach, which was where they'd run into Judith. It wasn't exactly an encounter they'd sought. In fact, as much as Pansy loved her sisters, their arrival this morning, with Garth and Lou in tow, had necessitated the escape. Pansy and Rex quite simply wanted to be alone. So, after Rex had borrowed some fresh jeans from Garth, Pansy threw on shorts and a halter, and they'd headed out into the brilliant sunshine, holding hands.

It had been a very long night. Whenever they weren't making love, Rex had explained the awkward situation in which he'd found himself upon arriving on Seduction Island. Initially, he'd been unable to tell

Pansy who he was because of Judith. Later, one thing had led to another.

And now they wanted to enjoy each others' company, as well as survey the damage and see if they could be of any assistance. It was a time to count their blessings, and today, of course, those blessings included each other.

There had been a lapse in the conversation, and now Judith turned to the couple, eyeing Rex a long moment. "I see you're back on the island, then?"

Not even Judith could sour Rex's mood this morning. And Rex had never really left. "Looks like it."

She frowned. "I thought I asked you to leave."

"There are no laws against a man taking a vacation, are there?"

She shot him a suspicious glance. "Is that really what you're doing here?"

"Of course."

Both officers knew better. Judith shook her head. "If there was any evidence, you know, the storm swept it away."

"If my father's alive," returned Rex cryptically, not about to let Judith in on what he'd found out, "I'm sure he'll show up soon enough. And with evidence," he added.

Judith arched a brow. "Evidence? Do you know something I don't?"

Rex shrugged. "My father didn't commit any crime," he assured, pushing a hand into the back pocket of the borrowed jeans. "I figure he stumbled onto something at Police Plaza and that he's working the case on his own, figuring he won't get any support from the brass."

Pansy's heart ached for Rex and the family he'd told her so much about. Surely, Rex was right, and Augustus had done nothing wrong. While Rex's disguise explained why his father hadn't come forward that day at Castle O'Lannaise, Pansy wished they'd been able to talk to him.

Looking as if she'd like nothing more than to pursue the matter, Judith exhaled a soft sigh that, coming from another woman's lips, would have been sexy. Coming from Judith, it was much like the rest of her—intimidating. "Well, like I said," she repeated, "any evidence is gone."

Pansy was getting the distinct impression that Judith would like nothing more than to see Augustus Steele behind bars. But why? Rex had hinted at the woman's inexplicable animosity toward his father and his brother Sullivan, and said that no one understood it.

Judith stared up the shoreline. Some of her men had brought parts of the *Destiny* back onto the beach for use at a forensics table. They knew the vessel was sabotaged, but they were still trying to determine the exact origin of the blast. Shifting her gaze to the white adobe of Castle O'Lannaise, gleaming under the hot sun of a cloudless sky, Judith mused, "That's the only place that wasn't affected by the storm."

"True. But there really wasn't much damage, given the severity of the storm," returned Pansy. "I grew up here, so I've seen worse."

Already, the beach was nearly clear of debris. Inland, however, things were worse. Much of the island was still without phone service and power, but very few residences had been destroyed. Once the French door was fixed, the Hanley house would be as right as rain, so to speak.

Judith's arresting eyes had settled on Pansy. "I've heard all kinds of things about that place. Some say it's haunted, and there are rumors that no one knows who owns the place. Not even you, and you're the Realtor."

Pansy wondered if Judith was fishing. Did she think the owners might be connected to the case involving Augustus Steele? Shrugging, Pansy shot Rex a smile. "Actually," she announced, "I think I've found a buyer."

Judith frowned. "Who?"

"Someone who wants to refurbish the place and open it as a resort," said Pansy, never taking her eyes from Rex. "But I can't really talk about the sale until the plans are final."

Judith's insatiable curiosity was piqued. "You can't even give a hint about what he does for a living?"

Pansy smiled. "Oh," she said, "he's by turns a poet, painter and chef."

Judith's expression was unreadable, but after a moment, she nodded as if the answer satisfied her. Suspicion returned soon enough, as she noted the physical closeness between Pansy and Rex. "What happened to that friend of yours?" she asked Pansy.

Realizing she'd been beaming at Rex, Pansy brought her attention to the conversation. "Which friend?"

"That really nice man you had over for dinner," said Judith. "You know, Ned Nelson, the architect."

"Oh, Ned," Pansy said, fighting another smile, her eyes twinkling as they met Rex's. "Uh, he evacuated," she said, "but...I believe he came back to get some of his things." Secretly, she was very glad to count herself as one of those things.

"In case I miss him," returned Judith, "please tell him I said goodbye. It was a pleasure to meet him." She leveled a cool stare at Rex, as if to say the opposite had been true in the case of their meeting.

"Will do," Pansy assured.

Moments later, when they were out of earshot, she and Rex collapsed onto the beach laughing, rolling in the sand until they landed with her on top. The surf bubbled, touching their toes, frothing on their calves as her legs fell between his. Pansy's laughter tempered to a chuckle. "I like knowing your secrets," she whispered, feeling the beginnings of his arousal and suddenly wishing they were inside where she could enjoy the benefits of it.

Rex smiled at her lazily, the look in his eyes reminding her of the first time they'd made love in the sand, not far from here, in the dunes. "Not all my secrets," he corrected.

She frowned. "Which ones are you withholding?"

"My plans for the future."

Her heart missed a beat. He wasn't leaving, was he? "Want to tell me about them?"

He glanced toward the tables on the beach where Judith's forensic team was working with the boat. When Pansy followed his gaze, she could see the splintered wood that read *Destiny*. She sobered. Last night, they'd traded stories, thrilling each other with the odd sights they'd noted during the storm, and while they'd never tell another living soul, both she and Rex were convinced that Jacques and Iris had found each other again in the storm. Chalk it up to their poetic natures.

A smile ghosted across her lips. It was a good thing, she thought. Now that Jacques and Iris were reunited, maybe the island's legendary storms would cease. No doubt, the tourist trade would flourish and Castle O'Lannaise would thrive. Especially if Rex stayed, bought the place and helped her open it to the public. "Would those plans include buying my castle?" she prompted.

"Of course. That went without saying."

"Oh?" She arched a brow. "And your other plans?"

"To marry you." He smiled. "You already said yes, you know."

"Sometimes," Pansy murmured, "things turn out right in the end."

"Sometimes people are meant to be," he agreed, his eyes meshing with hers, his cheek nuzzling her neck.

"Sometimes people stay together forever," she whispered. "Even eternity."

"*Destiny*," he murmured agreeably, his hands in her hair pulling her down for a kiss. "I've just got one question."

Her lips curled upward. "What's that?"

He chuckled. "Have I done what you wanted? Played your pirate and ruined you for all other men, the way Jacques did Iris?"

"Oh, definitely," she whispered. Swooping her head down, she kissed him, and as her moist lips began to move on his, there was no mistake about it. They were both ruined for all others. And neither minded in the least.

* * * * *

In August look for
another story of
seduction and intrigue
when you meet
Sullivan Steele in

THE PROTECTOR!

1

A month ago...

"YOUR FATHER'S GUILTY." Framed in the doorway with uniformed officers milling behind her in the squad room, Judith Hunt stood before him, her posture perfect, wearing a gray silk suit with a jacket most people would have removed due to the summer heat. Farther behind her, through a window, sunlight glanced off the jagged steel Manhattan skyline in hot metallic flashes. "You know it," she continued, surveying him through suspicious blue eyes, "and I know it, Steele."

Steele, Sully thought. She usually used his last name, probably because she knew it grated on his nerves; on the rare occasion she used his first, it was always Sullivan, never Sully. Standing behind his desk, he glanced down at the files littering the surface, his attention settling on a festive mug the officers had given him last Christmas. *To Captain Steele: The Great Protector,* it said, invoking Sully's nickname. The mug, when presented, had been brimming over with red-and-green condoms.

At least his men knew he was dedicated to ensuring safety. Realizing with a start that Judith was scrutinizing his possessions, Sully shifted his hazel eyes to hers again. He hated that he was reassessing everything now, wondering what conclusions she'd draw about him from the items, but he was glad the files made him look busy, which he was, and that she'd noticed the mug, since it showed his men cared.

The only thing Sully regretted was the ship in a bottle. Too personal, he decided. He'd built the ships when he was a kid, and he'd brought some into the office from a collection he'd otherwise divided between his parents' home and his downtown apartment. Built inside a scotch bottle, the English galleon had five raised sails, and it was from the late sixteenth century, with a sleek hull and low superstructure that rose toward a slate-and-teak painted quarter-deck.

She arched an eyebrow. "A pirate ship?"

He shrugged with a casualness he never really felt in her presence. "Doesn't that figure?" he inquired mildly. "After all, my father's a crook, right?"

"I'm not sure a pirate ship's an appropriate ornament for the desk of a precinct captain," she agreed calmly.

"I find flying a Jolly Roger very appropriate, Ms. Hunt."

"The Jolly Roger?"

"*Jolie Rouge*," Sully clarified, the French words feeling sensual in his mouth as he nodded toward the ship. "A red flag. They were meant to communicate that no quarter would be given...that any battle would be to the death."

"I'll take that under advisement." A heartbeat passed. "And thanks for the history lesson."

"No problem," he returned amiably. "Where better than a precinct to intimidate adversaries into surrender, to avoid costly fights?"

"Is that what you're trying to do?" she countered, her lips twisting into a challenging smile. "Intimidate me?"

He fought not to roll his eyes. If Sully didn't know better, he'd think the edginess of these encounters was due to Judith's attraction to him. She wouldn't be the first woman to be drawn to his large, strong body, or the cynical set of his square jaw, or the soft texture of his short, honey hair. "Would that be possible?"

"No. So, if you're trying, it's not working, Steele."

There it was again. *Steele.* He'd worked with Judith ever since her transfer from the city's legal department to the investigative unit in Internal Affairs a few years ago, and now, for the umpteenth time, Sully wondered what made such a beautiful woman distrustful enough to spend her time prosecuting cops.

And she *was* beautiful—if a man could tolerate her attitude long enough to notice. She was nearly six feet tall. The hair hanging just past her shoulders was such a rich, chocolate brown that it appeared black. Her eyes were blue or violet, depending on the light, and they popped from a pale oval face, framed by dark arching wisps of eyebrows. Her mouth, always lipsticked in crimson, was so remarkable that it had earned her the nickname, "Lips." No officer said it to her face, of course, but the name was well-deserved. Sully wasn't the first to wonder how that mouth would taste.

She was clearly fighting exasperation. "Aren't you going to say anything more?"

"Why bother?" Sully returned dryly, pushing aside the tails of a brown suit jacket so his hands could delve into the trouser pockets. He'd rolled down his shirt sleeves, donned the jacket and tightly reknotted his tie as soon as he'd heard Judith was on her way up to his office. "When it comes to Pop, you've already played judge, jury and executioner. What's to discuss?"

Her crimson lips parted slightly, just enough that he caught a flash of her perfect teeth, a sliver of velvet tongue. "The facts," she continued, oblivious to the effect she had on him. "Discussing those could keep us busy for quite some time."

Pulling his eyes from her legs, he said, "Given all the dirty cops you suspect live in this city, I figured you'd be busy enough without coming downtown to keep me company."

"Your lack of concern about my investigation into your father's affairs brings you under suspicion, Steele. And if you'll protect your father, Internal Affairs has to assume you'll also protect your men—"

"I am concerned," he countered flatly. "And nobody in my precinct's on the take, Judith," he added. He'd used her first name this time, and he was glad to see it grated every bit as much as when she called him Steele. Good. He'd keep using it.

She nodded curtly. "If anyone is, we'll find out."

Was she really going to use his father's disappearance as an excuse to crack down on his department? "Are you threatening me?"

Her eyes locked with his. "Should I be?"

"Are you?"

"I'm doing my job."

"And you're good at it," he admitted with grudging respect.

"If you think flattery will make me back off," she returned, as if he'd just confirmed every lowdown, dirty suspicion she'd ever had about him, "you've seriously underestimated me."

He'd done no such thing. He knew Judith Hunt's resume like the back of his hand—just as she undoubtedly knew his. "We should be working together on this."

She stared at him as if he were the most thoroughly dense man she'd ever encountered. "Which is exactly why I'm here," she said, not about to let him sidetrack her. "Joe wants—"

"Your boss is my father's ex-partner," Sully interjected, speaking of Joe Gregory. "They went through the academy together, then partnered-up in Hell's Kitchen." After that, they'd begun busting gangs and mobsters in Chinatown. Years later, when Joe wound up working in administration at Police Plaza, he'd brought Augustus Steele on board. "Joe knows he's innocent."

If she hadn't been privy to the previous connection between the men, she kept it to herself. "That may well be," she said, her tone dubious, "but Joe's the one who sent me to question you. He wants your father found—"

"I want Pop found, too," Sully replied, years of police work enabling him to keep the indignation from his voice. "Because *when* Pop's found, he'll offer the explanation that'll clear his name."

"I want him found—" Judith's blue eyes turned steely in a way that indicated she knew more than she was telling "—so that I can prosecute him."

"In this case, you care more about making a collar," Sully accused softly, "than about discovering the truth." He paused, taking a calming breath. "What information do you have that you're not sharing?"

"None," she assured.

"You're lying."

"Steele, your father was caught on videotape, withdrawing seven million dollars in public funds. He transferred the money from Citicorp, then picked it up at People's National in two suitcases. The money belongs to the Citizens Action committee—"

"I know that—"

"And the money's usually invested—"

"With determinations made by the Dispersion Committee about where to spend it." Sully's own precinct had benefited from the fund the previous year, getting allocations for new squad cars. "Why wasn't the money invested?" Judith might offer him that much, at least. "Why was it available for a cash transfer?"

"Because someone was planning to steal it?" she said dryly.

Cute. "Not my father," he assured once more. "My brothers and I are convinced he stumbled onto an embezzlement scheme at Police Plaza."

Her eyes widened in astonishment. "You think somebody other than your father was going to steal the money?"

Sully nodded, choosing to ignore her sarcasm. "We think Pop withdrew the money, then hid it, so whoever was planning to steal it couldn't do so." His lips set in a grim line. If there was anyone he'd trust to get to the bottom of his father's disappearance, it was her. She was rumored to be the best, not that he'd tell her that. "If you'd be cooperative..."

She merely stared at him, her gaze cool. "If you Steeles withhold information, I'll arrest each and every one of you for aiding and abetting a suspect."

"He's our father, dammit, not a suspect."

Their gazes locked, and Sully couldn't believe the ease with which Judith maintained eye contact. Most people withered under the stare he'd perfected for years. Calculated to unnerve the hardest criminals, the unflinching, penetrating gaze usually made people fidget immediately. Keeping his voice low, he said, "My father could be dead. You realize that, don't you? The *Destiny* exploded."

She nodded curtly. "We haven't found any bodies."

He knew that, too. Nevertheless, Sully's gut tightened. No one in the Steele family would rest easily until Augustus was found. Abruptly, Sully broke eye contact with Judith and circled the desk.

"I'd like to know one thing," Sully couldn't help but murmur, coming an inch closer, just close enough that she'd feel his breath and the coiled power in his body.

She was tall, but not as tall as he, and because she was looking up, her wary stare came through a fringe of wet-looking black eyelashes. He inhaled sharply, pulling in her scent. No woman had a right to be so beautiful, he thought vaguely, or to smell so good, especially not a cop from Internal Affairs. Much less, a woman who intended to prosecute his father, something that made her the enemy.

"What do you want to know, Steele?" she finally asked.

"What happened that turned you to ice?" His voice had inexplicably hushed to a whisper. Suddenly, he was fighting the urge to lift a finger and touch her face—maybe because the gesture would send her packing, or maybe just because he simply wanted to touch her, he wasn't sure which.

"Steele," she said, "I'm not made of ice."

"I said my father might be dead."

"I know that. And I have compassion for your situation," she added, her voice catching huskily. "I really do."

"Compassion?" he echoed. What did this by-the-book woman know about how Sully's mother, Sheila, was feeling right now? Did she know she was just five blocks away, pacing around the courtyard garden behind the brownstone where Sully and his brothers had grown up? "Compassion," Sully repeated dryly. "Oh, Ms. Hunt, I'm sure you've got it just the way they've got everything else downtown."

Her eyes turned watchful. "How's that?"

"In quadruplicates."

Her chin lifted a notch. What she said next seemed to cost her. "You're wrong about me, Steele."

They stared at each other a moment, and they were still staring, long after other people would have looked away.

"If you think of anything…" Her voice trailed off, and before he could answer, she turned to go, a whiff of soft female scent cutting through the sweat of the squad room. She was across the threshold when she looked back. There was something odd about how she did it, too, Sully thought, because she looked back the way a lover might, not an adversary. It was as if she had to make sure he was still standing there, watching her walk away. Her gorgeous crimson lips parted, as if she wanted to say something more.

He arched a whiskey-colored eyebrow. "Anything else I can do for you, Ms. Hunt?"

She looked at him another long moment, then shook her head. "Uh...no. But—" Her voice was unreadable. "Look, Steele, I'll let you know whatever I can about the matter."

Sully doubted it, but he nodded, anyway. "I'll call you if Pop contacts me." That, too, was probably a lie.

She offered another nod. Curtly business-like, it shouldn't have made fluorescent lights play in her dark hair, or intriguing shadows dance across her pale cheeks like whimsical phantoms. The things Sully was noticing about her at the moment had no proper place in a police precinct, either, but for a second—if only for the space of a breath—he was sure he and this woman were going to wind up in bed.

"I'll look forward to hearing from you then," she murmured.

"It's always interesting," he agreed, then added, "Happy sailing."

She quirked a brow.

"On Seduction Island," he reminded.

"It's work," she said, looking as if she was starting to have difficulty keeping her cool. "Not a vacation."

He wasn't sure, but as she turned to leave, he could swear Judith Hunt added a softly whispered, *Dammit, Steele.*

That brought a smile to his lips. He watched her go then—his jaw setting, his groin tightening, his eyes pulling down the length of her. Whatever happened, this woman would hold the key to information about Sully's father's whereabouts. And for the first time, Sully decided that was a perfectly good reason to seduce her.

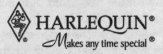

**What happens when a girl finds herself in the
wrong bed...with the *right* guy?**

Find out in:

#866 NAUGHTY BY NATURE by Jule McBride
February 2002

#870 SOMETHING WILD by Toni Blake
March 2002

#874 CARRIED AWAY by Donna Kauffman
April 2002

#878 HER PERFECT STRANGER by Jill Shalvis
May 2002

#882 BARELY MISTAKEN by Jennifer LaBrecque
June 2002

#886 TWO TO TANGLE by Leslie Kelly
July 2002

Midnight mix-ups have never been so much fun!

HARLEQUIN®

Makes any time special®